27

W9-ATY-425

Family Honor

Robert B. Parker

Family Honor

WHEELER
PUBLISHING, INC.
ROCKLAND, MA

★ AN AMERICAN COMPANY ★

Published in Large Print by arrangement with G.P. Putnam's Sons
in the United States and Canada.

Wheeler Large Print Book Series.

Set in 16 pt Plantin.

Library of Congress Cataloging-in-Publication Data

Parker, Robert B., 1932–.
    Family honor / Robert B. Parker.
        p. (large print) cm. (Wheeler large print book series)
    ISBN 1-56895-788-2 (hardcover)
    1. Private investigators—Massachusetts—Boston—Fiction. 2. Women
detectives—Massachusetts—Boston—Fiction. 3. Runaway teenagers—
Massachusetts—Boston—Fiction. 4. Boston (Mass.)—Fiction. 5. Large
type books.
I. Title. II. Series
[PS3566.A686F35 1999b]
813'.54—dc21
                                                        99-052174 CIP

For Joan: I concentrate on you

Their last months together had been gothic. Both of them had avoided being home, and the house in Marblehead with the water view had stood, more empty than occupied, both emblem and relic of their marriage. They had been much younger than their neighbors when they'd moved in, freshly married, twenty-three years old, the house purchased for cash with money from her in-laws. They had drunk wine in the living room and looked straight out over the Atlantic and held hands and made love in front of the fireplace, and thought about forever. Nine years is a little short of forever, she thought. She had refused alimony. Richie had refused the house.

Now she was carefully bubble-wrapping her paintings and leaning them carefully against the wall where the movers could pick them up when they came. Each painting had a FRAGILE sticker on it. Her paints and brushes were boxed and taped and stood beside the paintings. The house was silent. The sound of the ocean only made it seem more silent. The sun was streaming in through the east windows. Tiny dust motes glinted in it. The sun off the water made a kind of backlighting, diffusing the sunlight, and filling in where there would have been shadows. Her dog sat on her tail watching the packing, looking a little nervous. Or was that projection?

1

When she had married Richie, her mother had said, "Marriage is a trap. It stifles the potential of womanhood. You know what they say, a woman needs a man like a fish needs a bicycle." Sunny had said, "I don't think they say that too much anymore, Mother." But her mother, the queen of doesn't-get-it, paid no attention. "A woman needs a man like a fish needs a bicycle," she had said.

When Sunny had announced nine years later that she and Richie were divorcing, her mother had said, "I'm very disappointed. Marriage is too hard to be left to men. It is your job to make it work." That was her mother. She could disapprove of the marriage and disapprove of the divorce that ended it. Her father had been simpler about both. "You should do what you want," he had said of her marriage and of her divorce and of everything else in her life. "You need help, I'll help you."

Her parents were so strangely unsuitable for each other. Her mother was a vocal feminist who had married a policeman at the end of her junior year in college. Her mother had never held a paying job, and had never, as far as her daughter could tell, ever written a check, or changed a tire. Her husband had taken care of her as he had taken care of his two daughters, completely and without comment, which probably gave her the time to be a feminist. He was straight ahead and calm. He said little. What he did say, he meant.

He rarely talked about his job. But he would often come home and eat supper in his shirtsleeves with his gun still on his belt. Her mother would always remind him to take it off. The gun seemed to Sunny the visible symbol of him, of his power, as her therapist had pointed out during her attempt to save the marriage, of his potency. If that were true Sunny had often wondered what it meant that her mother wouldn't let him wear it to table. But it was never clear what her mother meant. It was clear what she wanted to mean. Her mother was verbal, combative, theoretical, filled with passion over every new idea, and, Sunny smiled to herself, sad to say, most ideas were pretty new to her mother. Her mother wanted to be a new woman, abreast of every trend, in touch with the range of experience from supermodels to theoretical physics. But she never penetrated any of the ideas she embraced very deeply. Probably, Sunny thought, because she was so desperately shouting, "See me, look at me." If her father noticed any of his wife's contradictions, he didn't comment. He appeared to love her thoroughly. And whether she loved him, or simply needed him completely, Sunny's mother seemed as committed to him as he was to her. They had been married for thirty-seven years. It was probably what Sunny had had in mind when she and Richie had talked about "forever."

Christ, didn't we fight over Daddy, Sunny thought, all three of us.

She leaned the last painting against the living room wall. She leaned the folded easel against the wall beside them. The furniture was gone. The rugs were up. The red oak floor gleamed. Without

3

anything in the empty rooms to buffer sound, the dog's claws rattled loudly as she trotted behind Sunny.

Sunny's sister was four years older than she was. God, she must have hated me when I was born, Sunny thought. It doubled the competition for Daddy. To win him, they had devised different methods as they had grown up. Her mother, impregnably married to him, persisted serenely in her noisy self-contradictions. Elizabeth, apparently convinced that nothing succeeded like success, tried to be like her. By default Sunny was left to emulate her father. Their mother dressed them both in pinafores and Mary Janes. Their father had built them a large dollhouse, and Elizabeth, with her long curls, had spent hours with it, manipulating her dollies. Sunny had worn her pinafores to the pistol range with Daddy, and while she was too female to be butch, she reveled in the androgyny of her nickname. And she learned to shoot. If one approach worked better than another, it was never evident. Her father persisted in loving his daughters as unyieldingly as he loved their mother. There was something frustrating in it. What you did didn't matter, he loved you whatever you did.

In the echoing kitchen, there were only the plates and glasses to pack. Sunny took them down, one at a time, and wrapped them in newspaper and put them in the cartons. The movers would have done it, but she wanted to do it herself. Somehow it seemed the right transition from one life to another. She was hungry. In the refrig-

erator, there was a half-empty jug of white wine, some Syrian bread, and a jar of all-natural peanut butter. She had some bread and peanut butter, and poured herself a glass of jug wine. Beyond the window over the sink she could see the rust-colored rocks stoically accepting the waves that broke in upon them and foamed and slid away. The dog pushed at Sunny's ankle with her nose. Sunny gave her some bread. Way out along the horizon a fishing boat moved silently. The dog ate her bread and went to her water dish and drank noisily for a long time. Sunny poured another glass of wine.

She had become a cop, the year before her marriage. Two years after her father was promoted to Area D commander. Her mother had asked if she were a lesbian. Sunny had said no. Her mother had seemed both relieved and disappointed. Disappointed, Sunny thought, that she couldn't martyr herself to her daughter's preference for women. Relieved that she didn't have to. Her mother had said, what about painting? Sunny had said she could do both. What about marriage and children? Sunny wasn't ready. The clock is ticking. Mother, I'm twenty-two. She remembered wondering if women needed children like fish needed bicycles, but she kept it to herself. The fishing boat had moved maybe an inch across the horizon. She took her wine and went and sat on the floor beside the dog with her knees up and gazed out through the French doors while she drank.

Richie was like her father; she'd known that even before she went to the therapist. He didn't say much. He was inward and calm and somehow a little frightening. And like her father, he was very much straight ahead, going about his business, doing what he did, without paying much attention to what other people thought or did about it. It was what he did that was one of the issues. He worked in the family business, and the family business was crime. He didn't do crime. She believed that when he told her. He ran some saloons that the family owned. But... she poured some more wine from the jug into her glass. There was a sort of ravine behind the house that ran down to the ocean, and the waves as they rolled into it sent up a harsh spray. Sitting on the floor she could see only the spray, disembodied from the ocean, appearing rhythmically above the slipping lawn.... It wasn't really that he was from a crime family any more than it was that she was from a cop family. It had to do with much tougher stuff than that and she'd learned early in their separation not to pretend that it was just cops versus robbers. A gull with a white chest and gray wings settled down past her line of vision and disappeared into the ravine and came back up with something in its mouth and flew away. Richie loved her, she knew he did. The fact that her father had spent a lifetime trying to jail his father didn't help, but that wasn't what felt so sharp and sore in her soul. Richie was so closed, so interior, so certain of how things were supposed to go, so too much like her father that she felt as if she was dwindling every year they were together, smaller and smaller.

"Dwindle," she said aloud.

The dog turned her head and cocked it slightly and pricked her big ears a little forward. Sunny drank some wine.

"Dwindle, dwindle, dwindle."

Her friend Julie had said once to her that she was too stubborn to dwindle. That her self was so unquenchable, her autonomy needs so sharp, that no one could finally break her to a marriage. Julie was a therapist herself, though not by any means Sunny's, and maybe she knew something. Whatever had happened they had been forced to admit it didn't work, after a nine-year struggle. Sitting across from one another in the restaurant of a suburban hotel, they had begun the dissolution.

"What do you want?" Richie had said.

"Nothing."

Richie had smiled a little bit.

"Hell," he'd said. "I'll give you twice that."

She had smiled an even smaller smile than Richie's.

"I can't strike out on my own at your expense," she had said.

"What about the dog?"

She had been silent, trying to assess what she could stand.

"I want the dog," she had said. "You can visit."

He had smiled the small smile again.

"Okay," he had said. "But she's not used to squalor. You keep the house."

"I can't live in the house."

"Sell it. Buy one you can live in."

7

Sunny had been quiet for a long time, she remembered, wanting to put out her hand to Richie, wanting to say, *I don't mean it, let's go home.* Knowing she could not.

"This is awful," she said finally.

"Yes."

And it was done.

Out through the French doors the fishing boat had finally inched out of sight and the horizon was empty. Sunny pulled the dog onto her lap. And sang to her.

"*Two drifters, off to see the world / There's such a lot of world to see.*"

She couldn't remember the words right. Maybe it was two dreamers. Too much wine. The dog lapped the back of Sunny's hand industriously, her tail thumping. Sunny sipped a little more of her wine. Got to go slow here. She sang again to the dog.

She wanted to be alone, now she was alone. And she didn't want to be alone. Of course, she wasn't really alone exactly. She had a husband—ex-husband—she could call on. She had friends. She had parents, even her revolting sister. But whatever this thing was, this as yet unarticulated need that clenched her soul like some sort of psychic cramp, required her to put aside the people who would compromise her aloneness. You lose, you lose; you win, you lose.

"You and me," she said to the dog. "You and me against the world."

She hugged the dog against her chest, the dog wriggling to lap at her ear. Sunny's eyes blurred a little with tears. She rocked the dog gently, *sitting on the floor with the jug of wine beside her and her feet outstretched.*

"Probably enough wine," she said out loud, and continued to rock.

One of the good things about being a woman in my profession is that there's not many of us, so there's a lot of work available. One of the bad things is figuring out where to carry the gun. When I started as a cop I simply carried the department-issue 9-mm on my gun belt like everyone else. But when I was promoted to detective second grade and was working plainclothes, my problems began. The guys wore their guns on their belts under a jacket, or they hung their shirt out over it. I didn't own a belt that would support the weight of a handgun. Some of them wore a small piece in an ankle holster. But I am 5'6" and 115 pounds, and wearing anything bigger than an ankle bracelet makes me walk as though I were injured. I also like to wear skirts sometimes and skirt-with-ankle-holster is just not a good look, however carefully coordinated. A shoulder holster is uncomfortable, and looks terrible under clothes. Carrying the thing in my purse meant that it would take me fifteen minutes to find it, and unless I was facing a really slow assailant, I would need to get it out quicker than that. My sister Elizabeth suggested that I had plenty of room to carry the gun in my bra. I have never much liked Elizabeth.

At the gun store, the clerk wanted to show

me a LadySmith. I declined on principle, and bought a Smith & Wesson .38 Special with a two-inch barrel. With a barrel that short you could probably miss a hippopotamus at thirty feet. But any serious shooting I knew anything about took place at a range of about three feet, and at that range the two-inch barrel was fine. I wore my .38 Special on a wider-than-usual leather belt in a speed holster at the small of my back under a jacket.

Which is the way I was wearing it on an early morning at the beginning of September as I drove through a light rain up a winding half-mile driveway in South Natick, dressed to the teeth in a blue pant suit, a white silk tee shirt, a simple gold chain, and a fabulous pair of matching heels. I was calling on a lot of money. The driveway seemed to be made of crushed seashells. There were bright green trees along each side, made even greener by the rain. Flowering shrubs bloomed in serendipitous places among the trees. The whole landscape, refracted slightly by the rain, made me think of Monet. At the last curve in the driveway the trees gave onto a rolling sweep of green lawn, upon which a white house sat like a great gem on a jeweler's pad. The vast front was columned, and the Palladian windows seemed two stories high. The drive widened into a circle in front of the house, and then continued around back where, no doubt, unsightly necessities like the garage were hidden.

As soon as I parked the car a black man

11

wearing a white coat came out of the house and opened the door for me. I handed him one of my business cards.

"Ms. Randall," I said. "For Mr. Patton."

"Yes, ma'am," the black man said. "Mr. Patton is expecting you."

He preceded me to the door and opened it for me. A good-looking black woman in a little French maid's outfit waited in the absolutely massive front hallway.

"Ms. Randall," the man said and handed the maid my card.

She took it without looking at it and said, "This way, please, Ms. Randall."

The foyer was very air-conditioned, even though the rainy September day was not very hot. The maid walked briskly ahead of me, her heels ringing on the stone floor. If her shoes were as uncomfortable as mine, she was as stoic about it as I was. My heels rang on the stone floor, too. The foyer was decorated with some expensively framed landscape paintings, which were hideous, but probably made up for it by costing a lot. Through the French doors at the far end of the foyer I could see a croquet lawn and, beyond that, a more conventional lawn that sloped down to the river at the far bottom.

The maid opened a door near the end of the foyer and stood aside. I stepped in. The air-conditioning was even more forceful than it had been in the foyer. The room was a man's study, and it absolutely howled of decorator. Bookshelves were filled with leather-bound books artfully arranged. The walls were done in a dark burgundy. The drapes matched the walls but with a golden triangular pattern in them. There was a fireplace that I could have stood upright in on the wall opposite. There was a fire in it. The ceiling was far above my head. There was a massive reddish wooden desk along the left wall of the room with Palladian windows opening behind it. The deep colorful rugs had been woven somewhere in the far east. A huge globe of the world was on its own dark wooden stand near the fireplace. It was lit from within. Above the fireplace was a formal portrait of a good-looking woman with smooth blond hair and the contemptuous smile of a well-fed house cat.

The maid marched across the rug and put my card on the desk and announced, "Ms. Randall."

The man behind the desk said, "Thank you, Billie," and the maid turned and marched out past me and closed the door. The man looked at my card for a little while without picking it up, and then he looked up at me and smiled. It was an effective smile and I could tell that he knew it. The little crinkles at his eyes made him look kind though wise, and the parentheses around his mouth gave him a look of firm resolve.

"Sunny Randall," he said, almost as if he were speaking to himself. Then he rose and came around the desk. He was athletic-looking, taller than my ex-husband, with blue eyes and a healthy outdoor look about him. He put his hand out as he walked across the carpet.

"Brock Patton," he said.

"How very nice to meet you," I said.

He stood quite close to me as we shook hands, which allowed him to tower over me. I didn't step back.

"Where did you get a name like Sunny Randall?" he said.

"From my father," I said. "He was a great football fan and I guess there was some football person with that name."

"You guess? You don't know?"

"I hate football."

He laughed as if I had said something precocious for a little girl. "Well, by God, Sunny Randall, you may just do."

"That's often the case, Mr. Patton."

"I'll bet it is."

Patton went around his desk and sat. I took a seat in front of the desk and crossed my legs and admired my shoes for a moment. Of course they were uncomfortable; they looked great. Patton appeared to admire them, too.

"Well," he said after a time.

I smiled.

"Well," he said again. "I guess there's nothing to do but plunge right in."

I nodded.

"My daughter has run off," he said.

I nodded again.

"She's fifteen," he said.

Nod.

"My wife and I thought somehow a woman might be the best choice to look for her."

"You're sure she's run away?" I said.

"Yes."

"She ever do this before?"

"Yes."

"Where did she run to before?"

"She didn't get far. Police picked her up hitchhiking with three other kids... boys. We were able to keep it out of the papers."

"Why does she run away?" I said.

Patton shook his head slowly, and bit his lower lip for a moment. Both movements seemed practiced.

"Teenaged girls," he said.

"I was a teenaged girl," I said.

"And I'll bet a cute one, Sunny."

"Indescribably," I said, "but I didn't run away."

"Well, of course, not all teenagers..."

"Things all right here?" I said.

"Here?"

"Yes. This is what she ran away from."

"Oh, well, I suppose... everything is fine here."

I nodded. To my right the fireplace crackled and danced. No heat radiated from it. The air-conditioned room remained cold. The windows fogged with condensation in which the rain streaked little patterns.

"So why did she run away?"

"Really, Sunny," Patton said. "I am trying to decide whether to hire you to find her."

"And I'm trying to decide, Brock, if you do offer me the job, whether I wish to take it."

"Awfully feisty," Patton said, "for someone so attractive."

15

I decided not to blush prettily. He stood suddenly.

"Do you have a gun, Sunny?"

"Yes."

"With you?"

"Yes."

"Can you shoot it?"

"Yes."

"I'm something of a shooter myself," Patton said. "I'd like to see you shoot. Do you mind walking outside in the rain with me?"

Other than the fact that my hair would get wet and turn into limp corn silk? But there was something interesting happening here. I wasn't sure what it was, but I didn't want to miss it.

"I don't mind," I said.

He took an umbrella from a stand beside the French doors behind his desk. He opened the doors and we went out into the rain. He held the umbrella so that I had to put my arm through his to stay under cover. We walked across the soft wet grass, my heels sinking in uncomfortably. Maybe there should be a new rule about wearing heels when I was working. Maybe the new rule would be, never. On the far side of the croquet lawn, and shielded from it by a grove of trees, was an open shed with a sort of counter across one side and a wood-shingled roof. We went to the shed and under the roof. Patton closed the umbrella. He took a key from his pocket and opened a cabinet under the counter and took out something that looked like a small clay frisbee.

"What have you for a weapon," Patton said.

I took out my .38 Special.

"Well, very quick," he said. "Think you could hit anything with that?"

There was a test going on, and I didn't know quite what was being tested.

"Probably," I said.

He smiled down at me.

"I doubt that you can hit much with that thing," he said.

"What is your plan?" I said.

"I'll toss this in the air, and you put a bullet through it."

If I did that using a handgun with a two-inch barrel it would be by accident. He knew it.

"I'll toss it up here," he said, "it's safe to fire toward the river."

He looked at me and raised his eyebrows. I nodded. He smiled as if to himself and stepped out of the shed and tossed the disk maybe thirty feet straight up into the air. I didn't move. The disk hit its zenith and came down and landed softly on the wet grass about eight feet beyond the shed. And lay on its side. I walked out of the shed, and over to the disk, and standing directly above it, I put a bullet through the middle of it from a distance of about eighteen inches. The disk shattered. Patton stared at me.

"I don't need to be able to shoot something falling through the air thirty feet away," I said. "This gun is quite effective at this range, Brock, which is about the only range I'll ever need it for."

I put the gun away. Patton nodded and

17

stared at the disk fragments for a moment or two; then he picked up the umbrella and opened it and handed it to me.

"Come back in," he said. "I'd like you to meet my wife."

Then he walked away bareheaded in the nice rain. I followed him, alone under the umbrella.

CHAPTER

2

Betty Patton was far too perfect. She annoyed me on sight in the same way Martha Stewart does. Her hair was too smooth. Her makeup was too subtle. Her legs were too shapely. Her pale yellow linen dress fit her much too well. She sat with one perfect leg crossed over the other in a low armchair in the study sipping coffee. The cup and saucer were bone-colored. There was a slim gold band around the rim of the cup. When Brock introduced us, she smiled without rising and offered her hand gracefully. Her handshake was firm but feminine. She said she was pleased to meet me. She called me Ms. Randall. I don't know how she did it, but any neutral observer would have known at once that Betty was the employer, and I was the employee.

"You've been shooting," Betty said.

"Yes."

"Can she shoot, Brock?"

"Well, sort of," Brock said.

"Did you ask Brock to shoot, Ms. Randall?"

"No," I said. "I didn't."

"Oh, well, you've disappointed him badly then. That was the real point of the exercise."

I had nothing to say about that, and I said it. The decorative fire was still burning vigorously. A servant must have fed it while we were out. The air-conditioning was still fogging the glass in the French doors.

"I think Ms. Randall is who we need," Brock said.

Betty smiled and sipped her coffee. She didn't spill a drop on her dress. She wouldn't.

"I rather expected you to think so," Betty said when the elegant cup was perfectly centered back in the elegant saucer. "She's quite pretty."

"She has a good background," Brock said. "She is straightforward. And I have the sense that she is discreet."

Discreet about what?

"Do you think you can find our Millicent?" Betty said, leaning forward slightly as if to make her question more compelling. Like her husband, she seemed incapable of an unrehearsed gesture.

"Probably," I said.

"Because?"

"Because I'm really quite good at this."

Betty smiled interiorly.

"Odd profession for a woman," she said.

"Everyone says that."

"Really?"

I knew it would annoy her to be clumped in with everyone.

"Yes," I said. "Usually they say it just as you did."

"Are you married?"

"No, I'm not."

"Ever been married?"

"Yes."

"So you're not a lesbian."

"Having been married doesn't prove it."

"Well, are you?"

"I guess that's not germane."

Betty stared at me for a moment. A perfect little frown line appeared between her flawless eyebrows.

"That's rather uppity, Miss Randall," she said.

"Oh, I can be much more uppity than this, Mrs. Patton."

She was motionless for a moment and then turned to her husband.

"I'm afraid she won't do, Brock."

"Oh for God's sake, Betty. Maybe you could stop being a bitch for a minute."

Again Betty was motionless. Then she put her cup and saucer on the coffee table, and rose effortlessly, the way a dancer might, and walked from the room without another word. I watched her husband watch her go. There was nothing in his look that told me what he felt about her. Maybe that was what he felt about her.

"Don't mind Betty," he said finally. "She can be difficult."

"I would imagine," I said.

He smiled. "She'd have preferred someone less attractive."

"I'm trying," I said.

He smiled widely. "And failing, may I say."

I nodded. "Your daughter's name is Millicent?"

"Yes—Millie."

"When did she disappear?"

"She hasn't disappeared," Patton said. "She's run off."

"When did she run off?"

"Ah, today is Wednesday," he leaned forward and looked at the calendar on his desk. "She went not this past Monday, but, ah, a week ago Monday."

"Ten days?" I said.

"Yes. I know it seems long, but, well, we weren't too worried at first."

"She's done this before," I said.

"Well, in a sense, that is, she's gone off to stay with a friend for a couple of days."

"Without telling you."

"You know how rebellious teenagers are," he said.

"I'm not judging your daughter or you, Mr. Patton. I'm trying to find a place to start."

"I have a picture," he said.

He took a manila envelope out of his desk drawer, and handed it across to me. I took the picture out and looked at it. It was a good picture, not one of those bright-colored school photos in the cardboard folders that I used to bring home every year. It showed a pretty girl, perhaps fifteen, with straight blond hair and her mother's even features. There was no sign of life in the picture. Her eyes were blank. She seemed to be wearing her face like a mask.

"Pretty, isn't she," he said.

"Yes. This a good likeness?"

"Of course, why do you ask?"

"Well, just that sometimes people look a little more, ah, relaxed in real life, than they do in studio photographs."

"That's a good likeness of Millie," he said.

"May I keep this?"

"Of course."

"You know what she was wearing when she left?"

"No, I'm sorry, she had so many clothes."

"Take anything with her?"

He shook his head, with that false help-lessness men like to adopt when talking about women.

"And have you any suggestion where I should start?"

"You might ask at the school?"

"Which is?"

"Pinkett School," he said. "In Belmont. The headmistress is Pauline Plum."

Pauline Plum. From Pinkett. How darling.

3

"What was he like?" Julie said.

Behind Julie, the light was slanting into my loft from the South Boston waterfront. It came in through the big window at the east end, and splashed over my easel, making an elongated Ichabod Crane shadow on the floor. Just out of the shadow, in the warmest part of the sunlight, my bull terrier, Rosie, was lying on her back with her feet in the air and her head lolled over so she could keep an almond-shaped eye on our breakfast.

"Tall, cute little crow's-feet around the eyes," I said. "Great hair."

"Nice?"

"A little impressed with himself."

"But you liked him?"

"Not much," I said.

Julie took a bite of her sesame seed bagel and a sip of her coffee.

"Money?"

"It would seem so. Huge house, servants, a croquet lawn, trap shooting, river view."

"In South Natick?"

"There's still land left there," I said. "This is a very big property."

Rosie got up and came over and sat the way bull terriers do with her tail balancing the back of her and her butt several inches from the ground. She looked steadily at me now, her narrow black eyes implacable in their desire for a bite. I broke off a piece of bagel and handed it to her.

"How about the wife?"

I had a mouthful of coffee and couldn't answer so I just shook my head.

"We don't like the wife," Julie said.

I swallowed the coffee.

"No, we don't," I said. "Arrogant, impeccable, condescending."

"God, I hate impeccable," Julie said. "They get along?"

"Maybe not. I almost had the sense she was jealous of me."

"Oh ho," Julie said. "He seem interested in you?"

"He might have been."

"Well, that's not so bad. Tall, crinkly, rich, and interested."

"And married."

"That doesn't have to be an obstacle," Julie said.

"It is to you."

"Well yes, but Michael and I get along," Julie said. "And even if I wanted to cheat I'd have to get a baby-sitter."

Julie was always eager for me to have an affair, I think, so she could hear about it afterward.

"How is life among the rug rats?" I said.

"Mikey has discovered that if he doesn't eat I go crazy."

"It's good to have a resourceful kid."

"The little bastard won't eat anything but macaroni with butter on it."

"So?"

"So it's not balanced."

"Oh hell," I said. "People live quite well on a lot worse."

"He needs protein and vegetables."

"Maybe he sneaks some when you're not looking. You're the psychiatric social worker," I said. "What would you say to someone about that?"

"That it's one of the few areas where he can exercise control," Julie said. "I can't force him to eat."

I nodded encouragingly.

"Like toilet training," Julie said.

"Didn't you have trouble toilet-training him?" I said.

"So what do I tell the pediatrician when she tells me he's malnourished."

"Tell her he'll get over it," I said.

"Oh sure. It's easy... you haven't got any children."

"All I did was ask a couple of questions. Besides, I have Rosie."

"Whom you spoil horrendously."

"So?" I said. "Your point?"

Julie finished her sandwich. "I can't wait," she started.

And I finished for her, "Until you have kids!"

We both laughed.

"The mother's curse," Julie said. "How old is this girl you're looking for?"

"Fifteen," I said.

We were through breakfast and putting the dishes into the dishwasher.

"Pretty?"

"Come on down to the office," I said, "I'll show you her picture."

The kitchen was in the middle of the loft. Behind it was my bedroom. The east end was where I painted. The west end was my office. Julie and I stood near my desk looking down at the picture of Millicent Patton. Rosie followed us and flopped down behind me. I knew she was annoyed. She never understood why I couldn't just stay still near where she was sleeping.

"Well, at least she doesn't have purple hair and a ring in her nose," Julie said.

"At least not in the picture," I said.

"If things are good at home," Julie said, "kids don't run away."

"True," I said. "But what defines bad at home will vary a lot from kid to kid."

"So where will you start looking for this little girl?" Julie said.

"Do the easy things first," I said. "Call the local police to see if they've picked up a juvenile that might be Millicent or found any unidentified bodies that might be Millicent."

Julie shook her head as if to make the thought go away.

"Have you done that?"

"Yes. No one fits."

"Good. Now what?"

"Where do young girls usually end up when they run away from home?"

"Prostitution," Julie said.

I nodded.

"You say that to her parents?"

"No."

"What if you find her and she doesn't want to leave?"

"I'll urge her," I said.

"What if there's a pimp?"

"There's almost always a pimp," I said.

"Maybe you should ask Richie to go with you."

"I can't do this work if I have to ask my ex-husband to protect me."

In the quiet I could hear some of the trucks grinding along Congress Street in low gear as they hauled stuff to or from the new tunnel site.

"I have never understood why you do this work, anyway," Julie said.

"I know," I said.

"Maybe if you gave me a reasonable explanation..."

"It pays for my painting."

"Shouldn't the painting pay for itself?" Julie said.

"Day at a time," I said. "It also pays for my MFA."

"Which you've been pursuing since I was childless."

"Night at a time," I said.

"Sunny," she said. "I've known you all my life and I don't understand you."

"At least you know it," I said.

Julie looked at her watch.

"My God," she said, "I'm late, late. I love you, babe, you know that."

"I love you, too, Jule."

We hugged. She left. I stared at Millicent's picture for a while. Then I put Rosie in the car and went out to visit the Pinkett School.

4

Pauline Plum from Pinkett was everything the name promised. She was tall and slim and flutie with a prominent nose and the kind of clenched-molar WASP drawl that girls used to acquire at Smith and Mount Holyoke. She was wearing one of those hideous print prairie dresses that are equally attractive on girls, women, and cattle. She made a point to introduce herself as Miss Plum.

We talked in her office, on the first floor of the Pinkett School's white clapboard main building, me in a maple captain's chair with a small plaid cushion on it, Miss Plum sitting straight in her high-backed leather swivel, with her feet on the floor and her hands folded before her on the desktop.

"Millicent Patton is not a very industrious student," she said.

"How so?"

"She is bright enough, at least she seems so. But she also seemed to lack any motivation."

"Bad grades?"

"Yes, but more than that. She isn't active in school affairs. She doesn't play a sport. She is not on the yearbook staff, she has no extracurricular activities on her transcript."

"She is not a resident," I said.

"No, we are not a resident school."

"Any special friends here?"

"Sadly, none that I know of."

"No friends that she might have gone to visit without telling her parents?"

"None."

"Could she have friends you don't know about?" I said.

"Possibly," Miss Plum said. "But I keep a close eye on my charges, and after you called I made it a point to refamiliarize myself with Millicent and her situation."

"No boyfriends?"

"This is a girls' school."

"Doesn't mean she might not have a boyfriend," I said.

"We feel dating is better left to later years," Miss Plum said. "We try to focus our girls on growing into accomplished young ladies."

"And I'll bet you do a hell of a job," I said.

Miss Plum frowned. Accomplished young ladies did not speak that way.

"Our graduates usually continue their education at the best schools," she said.

"Where do you suppose Millicent Patton is headed?"

"I fear that perhaps a public junior college would be her only option," Miss Plum said.

"Eek," I said.

"Did you go to college, Miss Randall?"

"Yes."

I knew Miss Plum was dying to know where, but I was too perverse to tell her, and she was too well-bred to ask. I'd known a lot of Miss Plums, people who couldn't form an opinion of you until they knew where you went to college, and what your father or husband did for a living, and where you grew up. I was sure in Miss Plum's world that no accomplished young lady became a private eye.

"So what was wrong with Millicent Patton?" I said. "Why didn't she fit in? Why is she the one that won't go to a good school and has no friends and might end up, God forbid, in a public junior college?"

"As I say, she is unmotivated."

"That's not really an answer," I said. "That is just another way of describing the problem."

"What answer would you prefer, Miss Randall?"

"Why was she unmotivated?"

"I can't say. I can tell you that the failure is not at Pinkett. We have tried every possible way to encourage her participation in the educational experience here."

"Do you know her parents?" I said.

"Yes."

"And?"

"I beg your pardon?"

"And what do you think of them?" I said.

"I am not here to render an appraisal of Mr. and Mrs. Patton," she said.

"Do you think her home environment has something to do with her lack of motivation?"

Miss Plum didn't like this. No accomplished woman of any age running an exclusive girls' school talked about the parents of her students, especially if they were rich and influential and might make a bequest. On the other hand, if there wasn't a problem at home, then the finger of disapproval pointed back at Pinkett.

"Let me prime the pump here," I said. "I've talked with Millicent's parents. They seem very, ah, contrived. As if they were performing life rather than living it."

Miss Plum didn't say anything.

"They did not seem to get along very well with each other in my short visit."

Miss Plum smiled a little uneasily.

"Millicent was gone for ten days before they took steps to find her."

"Have they gone to the police?" Miss Plum said.

"No."

"Wouldn't that be the, ah, usual first step?"

"Yes."

"Why did they hire you instead?"

"They mentioned something about discretion," I said.

"Wealthy people often value that," Miss Plum said.

"So do poor people," I said. "But they can't always afford it. What do you suppose they wanted me to be discreet about?"

"Why, I assume, Millicent's disappearance."

"Because it's so shameful?"

"I don't know. Miss Randall, these people are your employer."

"Doesn't exempt them," I said. "This shouldn't be adversarial, Miss Plum. You must want Millicent found."

She was silent again, her head barely nodding, as she looked at her folded hands. Then she raised her eyes.

"I am," she said, "a traditionalist in education. I believe in Latin, grammar, and decorum. I believe in math and repetition and discipline. I am not much taken with theories about self-worth and maladjustment."

I nodded.

"But I believe two things about Millicent Patton. I believe that she has never been loved. And I believe that sometime this year something happened. Her grades and her behavior, never admirable, have declined precipitously in the last two marking periods."

"You don't know what that thing might have been?"

"No."

"You think her parents don't care about her?"

Pauline Plum took in as much air as she could and let it out slowly in a long sigh, and then fortified by the extra oxygen, she said, "That is correct."

I nodded.

"We agree," I said.

"But they have hired you to find her."

"Decorum?" I said.

Miss Plum shook her head. She had already gone further than she wished.

"I really have a school to run, Ms. Randall."

"Or maybe she ran away for a reason and they don't want the reason known," I said.

Miss Plum's eyes widened with alarm. She was far too accomplished to discuss anything like that with a woman who, for all she knew, might have gone to a public junior college. She stood up.

"I hope you'll excuse me," she said.

I said I would and she showed me out.

CHAPTER 5

It was 4:30 in the afternoon. Rosie and I had been to seven shelters. The eighth was the basement of a dingy Catholic church on Centre Street in Jamaica Plain. We were talking to Sister Mary John. Actually I was doing most of the talking. Rosie was working on Sister to rub her belly. Sister Mary John was apparently not a dog person. She paid no attention to Rosie. I thought about mentioning St. Francis of Assisi, but decided it wouldn't help me find Millicent Patton, which was what I'd been hired for.

Sister didn't look too nunnish. She was dressed in an Aerosmith tee shirt, jeans, and loafers, no socks. I showed her my picture of Millicent Patton.

"Yes," Sister said after a long look, "she was

here. All she would tell us was that her name was Millie."

"She's not here now?"

"No."

"Had she been abused?"

"Not that we could see," Sister said.

"She tell you why she was running?"

"No. We try to help, but we try to do so without prying."

"I have to pry."

Sister smiled. For a non–dog person she had a good smile.

"I know," she said.

"Why'd she leave?"

"She just left without a word," Sister said. "But here's my guess. Every day or so, Bobby Doyle, who's the youth service officer at District 13, comes down and brings some donuts and we have coffee and sort of talk over who's shown up and what we should do about them."

"And Millicent spotted him?"

"Not even him, I think. She spotted the police car outside."

"And she was gone."

Sister nodded. She looked down at Rosie who was being completely seductive under the table.

"What's wrong with this dog?" Sister said. "It is a dog, isn't it?"

I decided to ignore the second part of the question.

"She wants you to rub her belly," I said.

The prospect of rubbing a dog's belly seemed deeply unappealing to Sister Mary John.

"Why do you suppose she ran at the first sign of a cop?"

"Afraid he'd come to take her home," Sister said.

"Any idea where she would go from here?"

Sister shook her head.

"I assume that sooner or later a pimp will find her," Sister said.

"That seems the prevailing assumption," I said.

"And rightly so," Sister said.

"Any thoughts on why kids do this?"

"Not brain surgery, Ms. Randall—they don't like it at home."

"There must be more to it than that."

Sister leaned back a little in the folding chair she was sitting on, and looked at me more closely. I felt as if I might have asked a good question.

"Lot of people settle for the easy answer," Sister said. "Of course there must be more than that."

"So many of them run away from home and end up degraded," I said. "It's almost a pattern."

"Maybe it's what they deserve for running away."

"Excuse me, Sister," I said. "But no one deserves to be giving oral sex to strangers in the backseat of a car."

"No, of course not. I'm a nun, not a shrink, but I've seen a lot of these kids, and they have equal measures of defiance and guilt. The defiance causes them to run away, and the guilt helps them end up selling their bodies."

"So they can run away and get punished for it, too," I said.

"Maybe."

"Some of it must be economic," I said. "They haven't finished high school. They haven't got a social security card. They have no hirable skills. Some of them, perhaps, simply have no other way to stay alive."

"Things usually have several causes," Sister said.

"So what causes them to run in the first place, in Millicent's case, from affluence?"

"Whatever is in that home is intolerable to her," Sister said.

"Molestation?"

"Maybe. Maybe a situation which must be resolved and she can't resolve it. Maybe simply the way being there makes her feel. What I know is that kids don't give up a secure home for a desperately uncertain alternative simply because loving parents are firm with them."

"There's something wrong in that house," I said.

"You can bank on it," Sister said.

Rosie gave up on Sister Mary John and nosed my foot. I rubbed her belly with my toe.

"You save many of them?" I said.

"I don't even know. They come here. They stay awhile. They move on. Some straighten out as they get older. Some we get psychiatric help for. Some we may save with prayer. A lot of them, I would guess, we don't save at all."

"Hard work," I said.

"Brutally hard, sometimes," Sister said.

"You ever want to give it up?"

"I'm a nun," Sister said. "I believe in a divine purpose. I believe I am an instrument of it. I did not become a bride of Christ for the perks."

We sat in silence for a moment in the small basement room paneled in cheap plywood, sitting in folding chairs on either side of a card table, with the shelter's files stacked in milk cartons around the walls.

"And you?" Sister said. "You seem in an odd profession."

"My father is, was, a policeman. He's retired now."

"And you wanted to be like him?"

"Well, no, actually I got out of college with a degree in social work, but I wanted to be a painter. My father got me a police job to support myself until I sold my paintings."

"And you've not yet sold them?"

"Some, now and then, and I'm trying to get a Master of Fine Arts at night, and this work supports me while I do the art."

"You are no longer with the police?"

"Too hierarchichal for me," I said.

Sister smiled. "I often think that of the church," she said. "If you became wildly successful as a painter, would you give this up?"

"I don't think so," I said.

"If you became wildly successful at this would you stop painting?"

"I don't think so."

Sister smiled as if I had said something

smart. We were quiet again. Sister looked down at Rosie.

"What kind of dog is that?"

"An English bull terrier," I said.

"Like General Patton's dog?"

"Yes, only Rosie is a miniature."

"She looks rather like a possum," Sister said.

"No," I said very firmly, "she doesn't."

Sister shrugged and stood up and put out her hand. "Good luck, Sunny Randall."

I stood up, too. We shook hands.

Outside the church, walking to my car I looked down at Rosie.

"Possum?" I said.

CHAPTER 6

There wasn't much point strolling around Boston looking for hookers until later in the evening. So I went to see Spike, at a place called Beans & Rice, near Quincy Market, in which he was a part owner. It was open for dinner, but it was early and they weren't busy when I got there. Spike was in the back, a phone hunched against his ear.

"Ma'am," the maitre d' said when Rosie and I walked in. "I'm sorry, but you can't bring the dog in here."

"Shh," I said. "You want her to hear you?"

From the back, Spike said, "Dog's a friend of mine, Herb, let her in."

When Rosie heard Spike's voice she strained toward him on her leash. Herb looked a little uneasily at Spike and somewhat less uneasily at Rosie, and smiled at me, and in we went.

Spike hung up the phone.

"Out walking our armadillo?" Spike said.

He pulled a chair out from one of the empty tables and I sat down.

"Rosie is not an armadillo," I said. "Nor, by the way, a possum."

"I never said she looked like a possum," Spike said.

He dropped to his knees and let Rosie lap his face.

"Not a tall dog," he said. "You want some food?"

"No, I've eaten," I said. "I need to talk a little."

"Sure."

He took a soup bowl off the china rack near the kitchen and put it on the floor and poured water into it from a pitcher. Rosie drank some. Rosie was a very noisy drinker.

A woman in sandals and a print skirt, with an Instamatic camera hanging from her wrist, was at a table near us. She was sitting with a woman wearing a Black Dog sweatshirt that was too tight and a long-billed yachting cap that was too big.

"Waiter," the woman in the print skirt said, "I'd like to order."

"I'm waiting on her right now," Spike said, nodding at Rosie, "I'll get to you."

"Isn't it illegal for dogs to be in a restaurant?" the woman said.

"No, ma'am," Spike said. "You and your friend are fine."

The woman and her companion put their heads together and whispered. I assumed they were trying to figure out if Spike had insulted them.

"Sit here for a minute," Spike said, "while I swill the customers."

A large man with a red face joined the two women at the table. He was wearing green plaid shorts and oversized black running shoes, and an orange tee shirt. He must have recently gained weight because everything seemed a little too tight except the shoes, which didn't look as if they'd ever been run in. The women whispered to him, and when Spike walked to the table he looked at him hard.

"What can I get you?" Spike said.

"You just insult these ladies?" the man said.

"Yes," Spike said. "The special today is a chicken burrito with salsa fresca and black beans, for eight ninety-five."

The red-faced man stared up at Spike. Spike smiled down at him.

"Would you like a moment to decide?" he said.

"I don't think so," the red-faced man said, and he got up with the two women and walked out.

Spike went to the service station, poured himself a cup of coffee, and came and sat at the table with me. We were alone in the restaurant.

"That was my agent on the phone," Spike said. "He thinks he can get me something with the road company of *Cabaret*."

"He better," I said. "You're going to be fired here pretty soon."

"They can't fire me," Spike said. "I'm one of the owners."

"That's right," I said. "It's so hard to imagine, I keep forgetting."

"Entrepreneurship, babe. You need something?"

"I'm looking for a fifteen-year-old runaway girl," I said. "Any thoughts?"

"She got a boyfriend?"

"Not that I know of."

"Girlfriend?"

"Not that I know of."

"Cops find her body?"

"No."

"Try the shelters?"

"This afternoon."

"And they don't have her."

"They did. She left."

"Well, if they don't have her, and she's still around here, I'd say she's probably hooking."

Rosie rolled over on her back beside Spike's chair.

"She wants her belly rubbed," I said.

"Me, too," Spike said.

"But not by me," I said.

Spike gently rubbed Rosie's belly with the ball of his foot.

"No, but your ex-husband's studly-looking."

"I'll tell him you think so," I said. "If she's hooking, I suppose she's with Tony Marcus?"

Spike smiled at me.

"Sunny," he said. "Every whore in the city is with Tony Marcus."

"But Tony wouldn't know her."

"Does the president of GM know the guy that installs floor mats?"

"So what pimp might she be with, if she's hooking? Who specializes in runaways?"

"She white?"

"Yes."

"Maybe Pharaoh Fox," Spike said.

"Does he still work St. James Ave. and Arlington?"

"Not so much anymore. Mostly it's male prostitutes there. Pharaoh moves the girls around every night: convention, ball game, wherever the johns are, Pharaoh drives them up in a van and lets them out right when the crowd breaks."

Spike was still rubbing Rosie's stomach with his foot. Rosie was motionless in some sort of ecstatic trance. No one could stand to rub Rosie's stomach for as long as she wanted them to.

"Pharaoh's a bad sonova bitch," Spike said.

"You don't meet all that many pimps who aren't," I said.

Spike drank some coffee.

"I was you," he said, "I'd get your ex to arrange a meeting with Tony Marcus, maybe Tony can do something for you."

"Richie's not in the family business."

"He's not out of it either," Spike said. "Tony wants to get along with the Burkes."

"Well, I don't," I said.

Spike shrugged. He took his foot off Rosie's stomach and rested it on the floor. Rosie remained on her back, her flat-black watermelon-seed eyes staring up at Spike. Spike stared back down at her.

"I'm not rubbing your stomach again," he said.

Rosie stared up some more, her feet in the air, one paw bent. Spike put his other foot onto her stomach and began to rub gently.

"You going to go looking for Pharaoh? Maybe I should tag along," he said.

"To protect me?"

"More or less," Spike said.

"I can protect myself."

"It's like safe sex," Spike said. "Two protect better than one."

I shook my head. "I'll be fine," I said. "Besides, there's my savage black-and-white attack dog."

Spike looked down at Rosie, whose eyes were now slitted, her tongue hanging out one side of her mouth.

"Should work," Spike said. "You unleash her on Pharaoh and he'll fall down laughing."

7

I spent the week with pimps and hookers and an occasional john who thought I might be available. I hung out in Kenmore Square after Red Sox games. I was down near the Prudential Center mingling with the convention tourists. I wandered through Park Square, and along Charles Street where it runs between the Common and the Public Garden. I cruised the Landsdowne Street clubs at closing time, although it didn't look to me that anyone would have to pay for sex along Landsdowne Street. I strolled hopefully around the South End, but most of the action there was gay.

Time flies when you are having a really swell time. All of a sudden it was the Wednesday after Labor Day and I had no idea where Millicent Patton was. Tactical support might help after all, and I had a date with some that night.

Neither my ex-husband nor I was willing to give up on us entirely. We had dinner every Wednesday, which I looked forward to more than seemed reasonable. So did he. Neither one of us said so; we were very careful about giving mixed messages. But the conversation was always about us and always charged and exciting. At the end of the evening there was always the unasked and unanswered question of whether we might have sex again.

Which both of us wanted and, so far, neither of us dared. The uncertainty of the relationship seemed to give it a greater charge than marriage had.

"Remember," Richie was saying, "It's my weekend for Rosie."

"She's got new jammies," I said, "and she wants to know if she can bring her Lou Reed albums."

Richie smiled. It was always nice when he smiled. He had a big jaw and a wide mouth and I liked the way the parenthetic lines deepened at each side of his mouth. He poured a little red wine into my glass and then into his.

"Whoever the hell Lou Reed is," he said.

We were eating in Cambridge in a small Middle European restaurant named Salt. Richie had on a blue blazer and a starched white shirt with the collar open. He had good color, as if he spent a lot of time outdoors, and his neck was strong.

"Anything new in the saloon business?" I said.

"Same old thing, ever-increasing profits, wild success," Richie said, turning the red wine glass on the table. His hands were clean and strong looking. I always hated delicate hands on a man.

"You started with a lot of seed money," I said.

"Yep."

The waitress came with some cherry soup for each of us. I sipped my wine while she put the plates down.

When she left I said, "That was bitchy. I'm sorry."

"It's okay," he said.

"Whatever the seed money, if you are turning a profit you are doing a good job."

"Yes."

We ate some soup and drank a little wine. The restaurant was full. We were sitting close together at a table for two. The energy between us was almost tactile.

"You need any money?" Richie said.

"No."

"It's clean," Richie said. "It comes from the saloon profits."

"The seed money wasn't clean."

Richie shrugged. "Let's not dance that dance again," he said.

"No," I said. "I don't want to either. I'm okay money-wise. Thank you for asking."

"Selling any paintings?"

"A couple. Not enough."

"The sleuthette business is going okay?"

"Sleuthette?"

"You find something patronizing in that?" Richie said.

"Of course not," I said. "Any woman loves diminutives."

"Lucky for me," he said.

"Yes," I said. "I remember."

We laughed. Any expression of feeling—laughter, anger, affection—threatened to surge out of control when we were together. Life without that pounding kinesis was unimaginable. So was life with it. The waitress reappeared.

"Are you finished with your soup?" she said.

We both were.

"Was everything all right?" she said.

"Wonderful," Richie said. "We're just saving room for the entrée."

The waitress smiled and took our plates.

"Funny, isn't it?" Richie said. "We both love to eat, but when we're together we don't seem to have any appetite."

"These are not casual dinners," I said.

"Oh," Richie said, "you noticed."

"I noticed."

The waitress returned with pork loin for Richie and roast goose for me.

"You dating anyone these days?" I said.

"Yeah, several."

"Anyone serious?"

"I'm only serious about you," Richie said.

"That might not be the best idea in the world," I said.

"It's not an idea, Sunny. It's a feeling."

There was something thin-edged and sharp in Richie's voice when he said it. It reminded me of how dangerous Richie could be. He'd never been dangerous to me, nor did I think he ever would be. But he was so nice-looking, so pleasant in his dark-haired Irish way that other people occasionally misjudged him.

"Feelings can change," I said.

"Probably," Richie said. "But these haven't."

"I know," I said.

"Everyone I go out with knows the score. I tell anyone I'm dating, 'If I can be with Sunny, I will be.'"

"I know I can't imagine life without you,"
I said. "But I don't know how to live with you."

Richie nodded slowly. It was familiar ground.

"It's not just the family stuff, is it?"

"It doesn't help," I said. "My father's a
cop, yours is a mobster."

"And still my father," he said.

"Yes. And I'm a detective and you're..." I
shrugged.

"A saloon keeper."

"You carry a gun," I said.

"So do you."

"It's not just the family stuff, is it?" Richie
said again.

"No," I said. "Not entirely."

I shook my head. We were quiet for a
moment. Richie took in a big breath and let
it out slowly through his nose.

"So," he said. "How's the goose?"

I stared down at my plate while I came
back from where we'd been going.

"It looks good," I said.

Neither he nor I had taken a bite. Richie
smiled. We both ate. It was good. We were quiet
for a time.

"You want something?" Richie said.

"Why do you ask?" I said.

"I know you. I've been looking at you for
a long time. You want something and you
don't want to ask."

"God," I said. "You should be the detective."

"And betray my entire heritage?"

I smiled.

"So what do you need?" he said.

"The thing is," I said, "it makes me so damned hypocritical."

"You need something that I can do because my family's in the rackets," Richie said.

"Yes."

"Maybe not hypocritical," he said. "Maybe just inconsistent."

"And a foolish consistency..." I said.

"Is the hobgoblin of little minds," Richie said.

"Exactly."

We were quiet again. Richie looked at me, waiting. I looked at my dinner. I had only eaten a little of it. Too bad. It really was good. Richie had barely touched his food either.

"Let's eat someplace awful next time," Richie said. "Then if we don't eat, it won't be such a waste."

I smiled and drank a little wine. "I need a favor from Tony Marcus," I said.

"Okay."

"I'm looking for a fifteen-year-old runaway girl and I need to know if she's hooking."

"Chances are," Richie said.

"I need to know, and know where."

"What do you do when you know?"

"I go get her."

"What if she won't come?"

"I force her," I said. "There are better lives than hooking."

"Tony doesn't know every whore in Boston," Richie said.

"I know, but he knows every pimp."

"He knows people who know every pimp," Richie said.

"Same thing."

Richie was resting his chin on his fist. He nodded slowly.

"Her pimp may object."

"They do that," I said.

"Unless of course Tony spoke to him."

I nodded. We looked at each other. I knew there was the usual conversation hum and the gentle sounds of service in the restaurant, but he and I seemed to be surrounded by resonant soundlessness. I could feel my breathing.

"I can get you to Tony," Richie said.

CHAPTER

8

My date wasn't going well. He was a lawyer, maybe two years younger than I was, making his way through a big firm. I had met him in night school, during the midevening break. I was still chasing my MFA in painting. He was taking an art appreciation course. His name was Don Bradley. He was lean and looked like a tennis player, and wore good clothes. He slicked his hair back a little tight, but nobody's perfect. We agreed to meet for a drink in the late afternoon.

"What I can't figure is the professor," Don said when the drink order was in. "Sonovabitch won't let you take notes or use a tape recorder or anything. How's he expect you to learn any-thing?"

"Maybe he wants you to listen," I said.

"I listen but I can't remember half what he says."

"And look," I said. "Maybe he wants you to look at the art."

"But if I can't take notes how do I know what I'm looking at."

"Original reaction?"

Don laughed and shook his head.

"Yeah, sure. So you're a real painter, Sunny."

"I paint."

"Got a studio and all?"

"I have a loft in Fort Point, I live there and paint there."

"Live alone?"

"I live with a bull terrier."

"A pit bull?"

"No, a bull terrier. Bull terriers are nothing like pit bulls."

"Yeah that's what they all say," Don said.

The drinks came. A Belvedere martini for him. A glass of Merlot for her. Don drank half of his.

"You're with a big firm?"

"Yes. Cone Oakes and Belding on State Street. Man, they are working me to death."

"It must be hard."

"Hard if you care about getting there."

"Getting where?"

"To the top," Don said. "I want a part-nership."

"How's it look?" I said.

"Well," he finished his martini and looked for the waiter. "I figure there's twenty-four hours in every day and if I can't find something useful to do with twenty of them, then I don't deserve to get there."

"Four hours' sleep?" I said.

The waiter saw Don's plight and brought him another martini. Don grinned at me over the rim of the glass. He drank and put the glass down.

"Oh baby, oh baby," he said. "Four hours' sleep on the nights I don't have a date."

His smile got wider.

"Energetic," I said.

"You got that right," Don said.

We were at the bar in Sonsie where most of the patrons looked like the anorexic models in high fashion magazines. Men and women. I never knew why emaciated and angry was fashionable.

"What is your legal specialty?" I said.

He grinned at me again. He had on the power-broker uniform: dark suit, striped shirt. Bright silk tie with little golf tees on it. I'd have bet most of my loft that if he took his coat off he'd be wearing suspenders.

"Winning cases," he said.

"You're a litigator."

"Right on, babe. That's pretty good. Most of the girls I go out with don't know a litigator from a guy that draws up trust agreements."

"Maybe you should start going out with women," I said.

"Like you?"

"Sure," I said. "Just like me."

"Well, that's what I'm doing, Sunny. That's just what I'm doing."

He spent most of the late afternoon and somewhat too far into the early evening drinking Belvedere martinis, telling me about his most famous cases. By 7:30 he was sloshed. I thought about leaving, but I wasn't sure he could get himself home.

"You have a car?" I said.

He did.

"Why don't we go home in mine?" I said.

"I kin drive," he said.

"I'm sure you can, but so can I. Let me drive you home."

"You feel better about that, Sunny?"

"Yes."

"Okey baby dokey."

I got him to the curb and gave the valet my ticket and when the car came I got him into the passenger side. Bending over, I was glad I had decided against my adorable little slip dress. With a little prodding he remembered where he lived and I drove him there, a cellar apartment on the corner of Mass Ave. and Commonwealth.

I pulled into a hydrant space at the curb. He sat without moving.

"Don't pass out," I said.

He giggled.

"Not me," he said. "I'm frisky as a lamb."

He ran "as-a-lamb" together. We sat. Nothing happened. *You have to get out,* Julie kept telling me. *You have to date. You can't sit home wishing you and Richie could make it work.* I got out and went around and opened the car door for him.

"Hop out, Don," I said.

"Besh offer I had," he said and swung his legs around. I got a hand under his right arm and together we got him out of the car. Together we wobbled him across the sidewalk and down four steps to his front door. He fumbled the keys out and dropped them, and pressed his head against the door jamb and giggled some more. I found his keys and opened the door for him and together we wobbled into his apartment.

"Wan' a nightcap?" he said.

"No, thank you."

"You arn' going?"

"Yep, I am."

"Hey," he said.

I turned and started out. Don wobbled after me and put his arms around me from behind.

"Come on," he said.

"Let go, Don," I said.

"Un unh," he said. "Night's young."

He rubbed himself against me. I was amazed he could still become erect. I wondered if he could feel the gun in the small of my back. If he could it didn't distract him.

"C'mon, Sunny, lighten up," he said.

He started to maneuver me toward the couch. I took in a deep breath and let it out. I stomped one of my two-inch heels hard on his toes, and twisted as if I were grinding out a cigarette. He screamed and let go of me. I opened the door and looked back at him. He was hopping on one foot and saying "Bitch" and trying not to tip over, drunk as he was.

"Good night," I said. "And thanks for a lovely evening."

As I drove back to South Boston, I thought there might be worse things than sitting home wishing Richie and I could make it work.

CHAPTER 9

I sat across from Tony Marcus in the back room of a restaurant that Tony owned called Buddy's Fox. I was the only woman in the room. I was the only white person in the room. Tony had about him the kind of dissipated handsome look that Gig Young used to have in old movies, if Gig Young had been black. He also had the biggest bodyguard I had ever personally seen. It reminded me a little of the short men I'd known who owned huge attack dogs. Leaning on the side wall of Tony's office, like the threat of rain, Junior might or might not have been bigger than Delaware. He was certainly bigger than Rhode Island.

"You got some good advance notices," Tony Marcus said. "Richie Burke and my man Spike."

"Spike?"

"Yeah. He called me this morning."

"Spike gets around," I said.

"He do," Marcus said.

"You still married to Richie?"

"Nope."

Marcus smiled and looked at Junior.

"Amicable divorce," he said to Junior.

Junior didn't look as if he knew what amicable meant. He also didn't look like he cared. Tony leaned back in his chair and checked to see that the proper amount of French cuff showed under the sleeves of his blue suit.

"So you're looking for a whore, Miss Sunny?"

"Fifteen-year-old runaway," I said.

Tony smiled. "That may be what she used to be, she on the street now, she's a whore."

"Either way," I said. "I'd like to find her."

"Why?"

"I've been hired to."

"So you really a detective," Tony said.

"Un huh."

"You don't look much like a detective," he said.

"You don't look much like a pimp," I said.

Tony laughed.

"Feisty," Tony said to Junior.

Junior nodded.

"Calling me a pimp," Tony said, "like calling Henry Ford an auto worker."

"Think you can help me find this kid?" I said.

"Sure," Tony said, "she hooking, I can find her."

"And if she isn't you'll know?"

" 'Less she hooking in East Long-fucking-meadow or someplace."

"Probably not," I said.

"She hooking east of Springfield, I can find her. Worcester, Lynn, Lawrence, Lowell, New Bedford, Fall River, she be one of mine."

"Not Springfield?" I said just to be saying something. Guys like Tony Marcus like to talk. Especially to women.

"Springfield belongs to Hartford," Tony said. "The Spices run it."

"So how shall we do this?"

"You think I'm going to do something?"

"I assume you didn't get me in here to tell me no personally," I said.

Tony grinned.

"Knew your father, you know that?"

"No."

"Never busted me," Tony said. "Sonova bitch tried hard enough."

"I didn't know he worked vice," I said.

"When he after me he working homicide," Tony said.

That was to scare me in case Junior hadn't already scared me. I remained calm.

"So how we going to find Millicent Patton?"

"You got a picture?" Tony said.

I'd had copies made of the one her father had given me. I produced one. Tony looked at it, and nodded slowly.

"She'll make some money," he said.

"Will she keep any?"

" 'Course not," Tony said without looking up from the picture.

I waited. After a time Tony handed the picture to Junior.

"Have some copies made," he said. "Circulate them. Let me know if we got her and who her pimp is."

Junior took the picture and continued to stand against the wall. Tony winked at me.

"Junior," he said. "I think I be safe with Sunny Randall here, while you go out and get that picture started."

"She ain't been searched," Junior said.

"I going to risk it," Tony said. "Go ahead."

Junior looked at me for a minute, then nodded and went out of the office. Tony leaned far back in his big high-backed leather swivel chair and put his feet up on the desk. His loafers had gold chains on them.

"I'm a pretty bad man," he said.

"I heard that," I said.

"A lot of women wouldn't want to come here alone."

"Lot of people," I said.

He laughed.

"Ah," he said, "a fucking feminist."

"That may be an oxymoron," I said.

"You ain't scared?"

"Not yet," I said.

"Maybe you just covering up," Tony said.

"Maybe."

He shook his head.

"Naw. Seen too many scared people in my time to be fooled. You ain't scared."

"You have no reason to harm me," I said.

"Not so far," he said.

58

"And I know you don't want trouble with the Burkes."

"Don't need trouble with anybody," he said. "Making a good living."

"See?"

He smiled again.

"If I decided I wanted to harm you, maybe you be scared."

"Why don't we wait until that happens," I said. "Then we'll know."

"I going to help you with this, Sunny. Richie asked me. Spike asked me. So I'll help. But don't make no mistake about me."

"No mistakes," I said. "I understand why you'd accommodate Richie, but why Spike?"

Tony smiled again.

"I like Spike," he said.

"I didn't know people as bad as you liked anyone."

"Sure we do," Tony said. "We just don't let it interfere."

CHAPTER 10

The only show I ever had was in a small gallery on South Street. The *Globe* art critic said I was "a primitivist with strong repre-sentational impulses." I didn't sell many paintings, but I was pleased to know that I had a definition. Standing now in the studio end of my loft, using the morning sun for light, I wondered if maybe primitive was just another way of saying amateurish. I was working in oils, trying to paint a view of Chinatown along Tyler Street. I never had time to go to a place and set up, so I was working from memory and a half dozen Polaroids I'd taken. It looked like Chinatown. In fact it looked like Tyler Street. And the building in the foreground looked like the Chinese restaurant that you see when you stand where I had stood. But the painting wasn't right, and for the moment I couldn't quite figure how to fix it. I sometimes thought art criticism boiled down to indefinables like whether it was a complete statement or not. This painting was not. Most of my paintings weren't... yet. I tried deepening the colors, and stood back a little and looked at it while the sun coming in the east windows made the colors as exact as I was likely to see them.

"Primitive," I said aloud, "with a strong representational impulse."

I was learning, but it was slow. I still took courses, and I was going to get my MFA because I hate to quit things before they're finished. But I knew the MFA didn't have a lot to do with my work. I had to learn myself how to do my work. Other painters could sometimes tell me things not to do, but they didn't even know how, or exactly why, they did what they did. I'd never met one who could tell me how to do what I did. The rest of the classroom work was theory, and a review of criticism. It was interesting. I liked knowing the sort of Kenneth Clark stuff about how art both shapes and records the culture it comes from. But it didn't help me to get Tyler Street complete. I had to figure that out myself.

Rosie was asleep on my bed with one paw over her nose. She woke up suddenly and jumped down and went to the door. In a minute the doorbell rang, and Rosie did a couple of spins and jumped up against the door and barked, her tail wagging very fast. Normally that would mean my father or Richie. I went to the door.

I was right. It was my father. Unfortunately it was also my mother.

"Did we interrupt anything?" my mother said.

"No, I was painting, I need a break."

My father got down on the floor with Rosie and let her lap his nose. Since my father was built like a short blacksmith it was an interesting display.

"Oh God, Phil, be careful of your knee," my mother said.

My father had been shot fifteen years before, arresting a man who'd murdered three women, and his left kneecap had been shattered. An orthopedic surgeon had pieced it back together, and while he limped slightly and it ached occasionally, it was as durable as the right knee. I knew that. He knew that, and, I think, my mother knew that. But she always warned him anyway.

My mother and I went to the kitchen and I put on coffee. My mother had brought some raspberry turnovers. My mother almost always brought something. My father got up and came into the kitchen and picked up a turnover.

"Phil, wash your hands, for God's sake. How do you know where that dog's tongue has been."

My father winked at me and bit into the turnover. I had come to realize as I matured that one basis of their relationship was his ability to ignore her. If she noticed it, she didn't seem to care.

"Well, don't be coming around trying to kiss me with dog slobber all over your face," my mother said.

"I may have to, Em," my father said. "You're so goddamned irresistible."

We had some coffee and turnovers at my kitchen table with Rosie in continuous agitation for a bite. My father broke off a piece of turnover and gave her some.

"Phil," my mother said, "you shouldn't feed her from the table."

"Certainly not," my father said.

"How are your courses?" my mother said.

She liked to think of me as a graduate student. It made her seem younger and it was more respectable than being a private detective.

"Fine," I said. "I only take one a semester, all the time I have."

"Won't it take a long time to finish?"

"Yes."

"But doesn't it postpone when you can become a painter?"

"I think she is a painter," my father said.

"You know what I mean. I mean full-time."

"I may never do it full-time," I said. "I like the detective stuff, too."

"Well, that's foolish," my mother said.

"Because it's not proper work for a woman?"

"No," my mother said, "because it's not proper work for my daughter."

I nodded. My father was munching his turnover and giving some to Rosie and looking at my incomplete painting of Chinatown at the other end of the room. I wasn't sure he even heard my mother.

"I never had your choices," my mother said. I'd heard it before. I could have recited it with her, had I cared to. "My generation married and had children and stayed home and raised them."

But you, I recited in my head, *you have a smorgasbord to pick from.*

"...a smorgasbord to choose from," my mother said.

Damn, she varied it on me.

"You can be anything you want to be and why you would throw that chance away and settle for this silly detective business..."

Now she shakes her head.

She shook her head.

It's beyond me.

"It's beyond me."

"I like the detective business," I said. "My B.A. was in social work, remember."

"And you're so pretty, too," my mother said.

"You hear from Richie?" my father said.

"I saw him three nights ago," I said. "We had dinner."

"How you doing?" my father said.

"How should she be doing," my mother said. "She's divorced from him."

"You getting along?"

"Better than we did when we were married," I said.

My father smiled as if he understood that.

"The thing is," I said, "we are really connected, and divorce or not, the tie between us is pretty strong."

"Divorce cuts that tie," my mother said. "Don't fall for it. You don't need a husband, and if you decided you wanted one, why would you want a hoodlum?"

"Richie's not a hoodlum," I said.

My mother looked at me the way you look at a slow child. My father picked Rosie up in his lap and let her lap him some more.

"I like Richie," my father said, his face was screwed tight against Rosie's kisses. "He's straight as far as I know. I don't like his father so much, or his uncle, but they're stand-up guys."

"Whatever that means," my mother said.

"You working on something?" my father said.

"I'm working on a missing girl, a runaway, she's fifteen."

"Where's she from?"

"South Natick."

"You think she's in Boston?"

"That would be my guess," I said. "You don't run away from South Natick to Medfield."

"Richie giving you a hand?"

"He put me in contact with someone who could help."

My father nodded.

"You figure she's hooking?" my father said.

"Probably," I said.

"Oh for God's sake," my mother said. "Must we talk about runaways and whores?"

My mother hated it when my father and I talked business. I knew she felt excluded and I knew she was jealous that he spoke to me as an equal. Good.

"Well," my father said, "you need something, you'll call."

"Yes."

"We had an auction," my mother said, "raised nearly a thousand dollars for the couples club last month."

My father and I listened quietly to the details.

CHAPTER 11

Tony Marcus was having heuvos rancheros at a table in the back of Beans & Rice restaurant, which wasn't open yet. Junior was with him, and a thin jittery little cokehead named Ty-Bop, who looked like he might be twenty. Junior was the muscle. Ty-Bop was the shooter. Spike sat at the table with Tony, straddling a chair, his forearms resting on the back.

"You called?" I said to Tony.

"Sit down, Sunny Randall," Tony said.

I sat beside Spike who patted my thigh.

"Got your girl for you," Tony Marcus said.

"You make me proud, Tony."

"She's hooking for Pharaoh Fox."

"You heard it here first," Spike said.

I smiled at him.

"Pharaoh know about me?" I asked Tony.

"No."

"He prepared to give her up?"

"We didn't discuss it, Sunny."

Leaning against the wall, Ty-Bop seemed to be listening to music that no one else could hear. He tapped and bounced next to Junior who was motionless.

"Will you speak to him about me?" I said.

"Thought I let you do that," Tony said, and smiled.

I nodded.

"That will be the hard way," I said.

"Might be," Tony said. "Pharaoh like his hookers."

"Like a father to them," I said. "Wouldn't it go easier if you told him to give me the girl?"

"Sure would," Tony said and smiled at me.

I waited. Tony turned his attention to the huevos rancheros.

"But you won't," I said.

"Let you do that," he said again.

I looked at Spike.

"Tony's hard to figure," Spike said. "He'll

66

help you locate the kid because he wants to stay cool with the Burkes, and maybe because he feels like helping you. Tony's a whimsical guy."

"So why stop short?" I said.

Tony continued with his eggs. Spike answered.

"Because it amuses him. He wants to see if you can handle Pharaoh."

"And why does he want to know that?" I said.

Spike shrugged. " 'Cause he doesn't know it now."

"Is that right, Tony?" I said.

Tony smiled at me.

"Sure," he said.

Ty-Bop boogied to the beat of his own drummer against the exposed brick wall. A couple of waiters set the tables toward the front of the restaurant. Junior watched them blankly.

"Anybody can handle anybody," I said. "It's only a matter of how far you're willing to go."

"Might be the case," Tony said.

He was finished eating.

"Can you tell me where I might find the girl?"

Tony stood up.

"Pharaoh turn her out different places," Marcus said. "You a detective. You'll find her."

"Yes," I said. "I will."

Tony grinned at me as if he genuinely liked me.

"You go, girl," he said.

Then he nodded at Junior and Ty-Bop, and they followed him out of the restaurant.

"What the hell was that all about," I said to Spike.

"What I said," Spike answered. "He's never met a female detective. I think he wants to see if you can cut it."

"Just to amuse himself?"

"Maybe Tony's not a feminist," Spike said.

"More's the shame," I said.

"I could trail along with you," Spike said.

"I thought gay guys were supposed to be sissies," I said.

"Growing up gay is a toughening process," Spike said.

"You'd stand up to Pharaoh Fox for me?"

"Sure."

"Thank you, Spike. But I can do this myself."

"I'm sure you can," Spike said. "How far you willing to go?"

I grinned at him. "All the way," I said.

"Heard that about you," Spike said.

CHAPTER

12

One of the things I had learned about Julie in the time that had passed since freshman year, when we roomed together, was that in her professional life, she was by reputation a good and wise counselor. Her personal self was an hysteric. For reasons having to do probably with my own perversity, I had always liked that about her. The hysteria was on full display at her son Michael's sixth birthday party, to which Rosie and I had been reluctant invitees. And we were the cream of the crop.

Others included five other children, aged six or less, bundled up because it was really too cold to have an outside party, but Michael had wanted a pony. There were also a couple of mothers, who seemed as hysterical as Julie, a bored pony, and a guy dressed up in a clown suit who was leading the pony around.

We were on Julie's front lawn in the suburbs. There was a card table set up with a yellow paper table covering taped onto it. The wind kept tearing the flappy edges of it. There was maybe a third of a chocolate birthday cake on the table, and a carton of half-melted vanilla ice cream. Several children, including Michael, were afraid of the pony. Michael was also afraid of the clown.

"Who wants a ride?" Julie said.

The grim cheerfulness she was grinding out made her voice reach registers I didn't know she had. Rosie was sitting in my lap. She didn't like small children any more than I did, but she was more genuine about it. A little girl in a pink dress came over and poked her in the ribs. Rosie growled. The little girl went immediately to Julie.

"That dog wants to bite me," she said.

Julie smiled maniacally.

"Nice doggie," she said, "Rosie's a nice doggie."

"I wish to bite her also," I said to Julie. "Where's Michael senior?"

"Off with the other two, this is just Mikey's day."

"And a dandy one," I said.

Julie did something with her lips that might have been a smile, and shook her head quickly. The pony made a deposit on the lawn, and Julie left me to attend to that.

A small boy who had apparently misunderstood the chocolate cake, and given himself a facial with it, came over with the little girl at whom Rosie had growled. The little girl hung back.

"Does that dog bite?" he says.

"Yes." I said.

"Bad dog," the boy said.

"She's neither bad nor good," I said. "She's a dog."

"Huh?"

I could feel the hair stiffen along Rosie's back. Her taste was impeccable. Julie appeared from the garage with a snow shovel and a plastic bag.

"Oh, look at Michael's mommy," I said. "Maybe you could help her shovel."

Both kids screamed in horror at the idea of shoveling pony poop. But they went on to watch.

The guy in the clown suit said, "Okay, kids, who wants to ride Pepe the pony?"

The kids hung back. One mother attempted to put her son on it, and he kicked and fought her until she gave up. Julie got her pony droppings into her green plastic bag and carried it over to the garage. The guy in the clown suit bent over and spoke to Michael in a voice that was apparently clownspeak.

"How about the birthday boy, he gets the first ride."

"Don't do that," I said.

But I was too late. The guy in the clown suit picked Michael up and plunked him on the animal. Michael was on the pony he feared, having been placed there by the clown he feared more. He screamed. It scared the pony, who bucked, which annoyed Rosie, who barked. I put Rosie down, held her leash in my left hand, stepped sideways toward the pony who was kicking his hind feet lethargically, and scooped Michael off with my right arm. Julie came out of the garage and across the lawn on a dead run. Michael was screaming, crying, and, incidentally, trying to kick me. Rosie was in full bark at the pony now, straining at her leash, thirty-one pounds of barely (and fortunately) restrained ferocity. Julie grabbed Michael away from me, and held him.

"What happened, honey. What happened, Mommy's here, what happened?"

Michael cried harder, and hung onto his mother. The guy in the clown suit didn't seem to have a good read on things. He was leaning down speaking in his clown voice to Michael.

"What's the matter? Is you scared of old Mister Bubbles?"

"Be better if Mister Bubbles stepped back a little," I said.

Julie focused on me over Michael's shoulder.
"What happened?"

"Mister Bubbles put Michael on the pony."

Julie stared at me, hugging Michael, patting his back. Rosie continued to bark at Pepe.

"Mister Bubbles?"

"The clown," I said.

"He put Michael on the horse?"

"Yes," I said. "Pepe the pony."

Julie turned her head slowly toward Mister Bubbles.

"You dumb fuck," she said.

"Nice language," Mister Bubbles said, "in front of the children."

"Fuck the children," Julie said. "Take your fucking pony, and get the fuck out of here."

"Hey, lady, you hired me."

"Out," she said, her voice soaring, "get the fuck out."

I got a hand on Mister Bubbles's arm and led him away. Pepe the pony came with him. He took no notice of Rosie, whose barking had settled into a low steady growl.

"She owe you any money?" I said.

"She got no business talking to me like that," he said.

"I'm sure Pepe was shocked," I said. "Have you been paid?"

"Yeah."

"Okay, pardner, then I think it's time for you and Pepe to mosey on down the trail."

He wanted to say something cutting, but it's hard to be cutting when you're standing around in a rental clown suit, and I think he realized that. He gave it up and took Pepe and headed for his truck.

When I put Rosie in the front seat of my car, and went back to the party, it was over. One of the mothers was explaining to Julie how Michael was just overtired, and everyone had really enjoyed it, and thanks for inviting us. Julie had disentangled Michael enough so that she could stand and say good-bye. He remained wrapped around her leg. There was a gathering of children, a strapping of car seats, a slamming of car doors and in a while it was just Michael and me and Julie. I went to Julie's garage and got a trash barrel and brought it back and began to clean up the cake and ice cream and paper plates. Julie sat down on one of the folding chairs that tilted clumsily on the uneven lawn and began to cry.

"I don't blame you," I said.

The crying turned to sobbing.

"Don't you hate parties?" I said to Michael.

He stared at me silently.

"I always did," I said.

"I can't do it," Julie said. "I try so goddamned hard and I can't do it."

Michael was no longer crying. He was very silent, standing beside his mother.

"Nobody can." I said. "It's not your fault, it's not Michael's. It's the way things work."

"Other people can have a damn party," Julie said.

"Not many," I said. "And you might not want to trade the skills you've got for the skills that make good party givers."

"I just wanted him to have a party like other kids."

Michael was very silent.

"In your enthusiasm for blaming yourself," I said, "you want to be careful that you don't spill some blame onto anyone else."

Julie raised her eyes and looked at me and then looked at Michael. She hugged him to her and talked and sobbed simultaneously.

"I love you, honey," she gasped, with the tears bubbling through her voice. "Mommy loves you."

I could see Michael's face over her shoulder. He didn't look as if he entirely believed her.

CHAPTER 13

I found her at 1:15 in the morning on Dalton Street behind the Prudential Center, handy to the big commercial hotels and the Hynes Auditorium. She stood near the curb just up from the motor entrance to the Sheraton, wearing white short shorts and heels and a sequined yellow tank top. *Clever outfit.* She smiled automatically when I pulled in to the curb. When I got out the smile went away, and she began once again to look up and down the street.

"Millicent Patton?" I said.

She stared at me and didn't say anything.

"My name is Sunny Randall," I said. "I'm a detective. Your parents asked me to bring you home."

Without a word she turned and started running down Dalton Street toward Huntington. Not wearing fuck-me shoes, I caught her in about ten steps. I got in front of her and put my arms around her and pinned her arms and made her stop. She made no sound. But she struggled steadily against me.

"Millicent," I said. "I will help you."

She tried to kick me, but I was too tight against her and she didn't really know anything about fighting.

"We'll sit in my car," I said, "and talk."

"What the fuck is this," someone said.

I let Millicent go and turned. Behind me was a tall black man wearing a six-button suit and a white shirt buttoned to the neck, no tie. He had a neat goatee and short hair. He was bony and strong-looking.

"Pharaoh Fox, I presume?"

"Who the fuck are you?" he said.

"My name is Randall," I said. "I'm a detective."

"Vice?"

"Private."

"Goddamn," Fox said, with laughter in his voice, "a private dick?"

I nodded.

"You can't be no private dick," Fox said. "Best you can do, be a private pussy."

He loved his joke, and laughed a lot harder than it deserved. In his presence Millicent Patton was motionless, perfectly docile.

I said, "Millicent's going with me, pimp boy."

Fox stopped laughing. His face was thin. The nostrils flared and his skin had a bluish tinge to it above the beard. He looked, in fact, a little like a pharaoh. He put his right hand into his suit coat pocket.

"Get off my street, private pussy," he said, "right now. Or I will cut you in fucking two."

One of the advantages of being a woman in this deal is that no one takes you seriously, so they are careless. While his hand was still in his pocket I took my gun out. I thumbed back the hammer as the gun came out, and put the muzzle up under his nose, maybe half an inch from his upper lip.

"Tell Millicent that she should go with me."

"Like hell," Fox said.

I bumped the barrel of the gun against his upper lip.

"I'm not a patient woman," I said. "And I haven't shot my pimp quota this week. Tell her. Now."

"You can't just shoot me on the fucking street," Pharaoh said.

"I'm a small blond cutie. You're a big ugly pimp. You'll be dead. I say you assaulted me. Who's going to take your side?"

He didn't move. He kept looking at me. There was nothing human behind his eyes. I didn't move. I could see the muscles tighten in his shoulders and neck.

"Go for it," I said. "Grab for the gun. Maybe I haven't got the balls. Maybe I'll hesitate."

I smiled at him.

"Or maybe I won't," I said.

Still he held on, the hatred flickering in his eyes like heat lightning. But I knew his grip was slipping.

"Let's find out, pimp boy."

He let go.

"You can have her," he said.

"Tell her," I said.

"Go with her," Pharaoh said to Millicent.

"Get in my car," I said to Millicent. "Pimp boy, you turn around and walk straight down to Huntington."

He backed away.

"What you say your name was, bitch?"

"Randall," I said. "Sunny Randall."

"Sunny Randall," he said.

I was in full shooter's stance, the gun in both hands holding steady on the middle of his body mass.

"Start walking," I said.

He turned and began to walk slowly away. I figured he didn't have a gun. He'd said he would cut me in two. Just the same I backed to the car. He was far enough away now that Wyatt Earp couldn't have hit him with the two-inch .38. I put it back in its holster, slid into the car and started up. Pharaoh didn't look back. As I drove past him he didn't look sideways. Then we turned left at Huntington and I couldn't see him anymore.

14

Millicent was sitting as far into the corner of the passenger seat as she could get, trying to be as small as she could get, and as quiet as she could get.

"We're all right now," I said.

We drove through Copley Square onto Stuart Street and turned left onto Berkeley. There were a couple of cop cars parked outside the old Police Headquarters. No one was on the street. There was no traffic. The mercury street lamps made everything look a bit surrealistic.

"You want to talk to me?" I said.

"About what?" Millicent's voice was small and hostile. She didn't seem to be feeling rescued.

"Why you ran away."

She shook her head. We drove across Commonwealth Avenue. The Back Bay was still. The street lights here were more self-effacing, filtered through the unleaving trees. A single bum slept in a pile of clothing on one of the benches in the mall. Millicent didn't speak. She stared straight ahead through the windshield. Her face was narrow, with a kind of incipient sharpness to it. Her eyes were black or seemed black in this light. She might become beautiful. Or she might not. It would depend, probably, on what life did to her, or what she allowed it to do.

"You like Pharaoh Fox better than you like your parents," I said.

"He cares about me," Millicent said.

"Like Colgate cares about toothpaste," I said.

"What do you mean?"

"He sells you," I said.

She shook her head. "He cares about me."

"He's a pimp, Millicent. He cares about money."

"You don't know him."

She scrunched up a little tighter in the passenger seat, an emblem of stubbornness, hugging her knees, staring straight ahead, her sharp little face closing in on itself. She was like one of those stars that implodes and becomes so dense that no light escapes. Across Beacon Street I went out onto Storrow Drive and headed west, with the river on our right. On the other side, the big commercial buildings in East Cambridge splashed light on the empty black surface of the water. Neither of us said anything as we drove along the river. We were behind B.U. when Millicent spoke.

"You taking me home?"

"I don't know."

We drove some more in silence. Past the Western Avenue Bridge she spoke again.

"How come you don't know?"

"I need to know what you ran away from before I take you back to it."

"What do you care?"

"Maybe it was worth running away from."

"How come you don't just do what they paid you to do and stop pretending?" Millicent said.

"I don't want to," I said.

Storrow Drive had become Soldiers Field Road. I never knew quite where that happened. We went past the Harvard Business School and past the Larz Anderson Bridge. I bore left at the light, following the curve of the river, and pulled into the park on the riverside opposite WBZ. I parked near the water, and shut off the headlights. I left the motor running, so I could have the heat on. It was cold at 3 A.M. in late September, and Millicent was wearing only shorts and a tank top. I gave her my jacket. She took it without comment and shrugged it around her shoulders.

"Why we stopping here?" she said.

She was getting positively chatty.

"It will give us a chance to talk," I said.

"Oh please," Millicent said.

I was quiet. The river was black and apparently motionless in front of us. It didn't look like it was moving past us, flowing east darkly, and without surcease.

"Why did you run away?" I said.

"I don't get along with my parents," Millicent said.

"Why not?"

"They're creepy," she said.

I nodded.

"You don't miss them."

"No."

"How about school?"

"I hate school."

I nodded again.

"I never much liked it either," I said. "You miss anybody at school?"

"No."

"Do you miss anyone at all?"

"No."

"Does anyone miss you?"

Millicent didn't answer.

"What do you think?" I said.

"About what?"

"Do you think there's anyone who misses you?"

"How would I know? My parents hired you to find me."

"Do you think that means they miss you?"

She was quiet again. But it was a different quiet. She was thinking about the question.

"No," she said. "It just means they worry what the neighbors think."

"Could be," I said. "Do you like one of them better than the other?"

"No."

"Do you dislike one more?"

"No. I hate them both."

"Why?"

"I told you. They're creepy."

"Give me a for instance," I said.

"My mother fucks everybody," Millicent said.

She checked me from the corner of her eye to see how I took the news.

"I bet that's hard to think about," I said.

"Don't you think that's creepy?"

"Maybe," I said. "Why do you think it's creepy?"

"For crissake, a married woman, her age?"

"How do you know this?"

"I know."

"How?"

"I see her come home sometimes. She's, like, drunk. Her makeup is all messed up. Her clothes are, you know, like crooked."

"This is suggestive," I said. "What's your father's reaction."

Millicent laughed a little ugly humorless laugh.

"He acts like she's not doing anything."

"Maybe he's right."

Millicent shook her head. She was eager now. Nothing like the chance to share grievances to encourage conversation.

"No," she said. "I found pictures."

"Your mother and other men?"

"Yes."

"Who took the pictures?" I said.

She was silent. I could tell she'd never thought about that.

"I think they maybe took them themselves."

"Sexual situations."

"Oh yeah," Millicent said.

"How'd you find the pictures?"

"I was snooping in her room."

I nodded.

"Your mother have her own room?" I said.

"Yes. That's kind of creepy, I think."

I shrugged.

"Your father know about the pictures?" I said.

"I left them where he'd find them."

"And?"

"Next time I looked they were gone. But he never said anything."

"Maybe he said something to your mother."

"No."

"Why not?"

Millicent gave me a scornful look. The scornful look of a fifteen-year-old girl is as scornful as it gets.

"He's scared of her."

"Why?"

"Jesus, you ask a lot of questions."

"I do, don't I. Why is he scared of her?"

"I don't know, he just is."

"Maybe he loves her and he's afraid if he makes her mad she won't love him."

"You think he doesn't fool around?" Millicent said.

Her tone suggested that she was trying very hard to speak clearly to an idiot.

"I'd guess he did," I said. "Does he?"

"Sure."

"It doesn't mean he doesn't love her."

"How can you love somebody and fuck a bunch of other people?"

"I don't know," I said. "But I know it's done."

"You married?"

"Divorced," I said.

"So who are you to talk?"

I wasn't talking. She was. I smiled at her.

"Sonya J. Randall," I said.

"Your first name is Sonya?"

"Yep."

"Gross," she said. "What's the J. for?"

"Joan. What made you run away when you did?"

"I told you, my parents are creepy."

"But you've found them creepy for a long time, Millicent. Why did you run now?"

She looked away from me and shook her head.

"There must be a reason," I said.

She continued not to look at me.

"I got fed up," she said. "That was the reason."

She was lying and I knew it, and she probably knew that I knew it, but there was no where to go. I'd already pushed her as hard as I dared. Maybe a little harder.

"If you think of another reason," I said, "I'd be pleased to know it."

Millicent didn't say anything. We looked at the river for a while.

Finally, without looking at me, she said, "I won't stay at home."

"You prefer sex with strangers?" I said.

"Being high helps."

I looked at the river some more. The black water moved effortlessly toward the harbor as it had in 1630. Except in 1630 you could probably drink it.

"Let's compromise," I said. "You don't have sex with any strangers for a while, and I won't drag you home."

She thought about that.

"So where am I supposed to live?" she said.

"With me."

15

I was talking on the phone to Julie. It was nearly noon. Rosie was sitting on my feet under the desk. Millicent was asleep on the floor at the other end of the loft on an inflatable mattress I kept for guests.

"She's staying with you?" Julie said.

"Un huh."

"Do you have any idea what a crimp that will put in your sex life?"

"How much crimpier can it get?" I said.

"It's already crimped?"

"Big time," I said.

"I'm crushed. I spent several minutes every day envying you."

"Spend the time finding me a nice guy who's good-looking and straight."

"You're after my husband?"

"Besides Michael," I said.

"Oh. I guess that's kind of hard. Have you met anyone?"

"A pimp named Pharaoh Fox," I said.

"Pimps can be fun," Julie said. "How long is she going to stay with you?"

"At least until I find out why she left."

"You don't believe she just got fed up?"

"No. She was lying about that."

"You're sure."

"I'm a licensed investigator," I said.

"Of course. How are you going to find out?"

85

"I'm a licensed investigator."

"You know, some kids leave home to punish the parents."

"I know."

"So that the more degrading and shocking their circumstances, the more horrified the parents are. And the more horrified the parents are, the more desirable the circumstances."

"Sort of like suicides," I said. " 'See what you've made me do.' "

"Do you like her?" Julie said.

"No."

"Why not?"

"I can't say."

"Because you don't know or because she might hear you?"

"The latter."

"Is she angry and hostile?"

"Yes."

"Hates her parents?"

"You bet."

"And every other adult."

"I'd guess so."

"Including you?"

"More or less, though I think there's some puzzlement."

"Because you don't give her the adult party line?"

"Something like that."

Julie laughed.

"You've never bought the adult party line yourself, Sunny."

"And my mother certainly has tried to sell it to me."

"So maybe you and, what's her name, Millicent, are a good match."

"I've got to be better than Pharaoh Fox," I said.

"Who?"

"The gentleman who represented her," I said.

"Her pimp."

"Yes."

"You know, there's one thing you ought to remember," Julie said. Her voice dropped a little as she shifted into her professional mode. "Some women rather like being whores, if the circumstances are not too degrading. They like the physical sensation, they like the easy money, they like the semblance of male attention."

"What's not to like?" I said.

"A lot, as you well know. But in many cases, these women are able to distance themselves from the actuality of their situation."

"And," I said, "in some cases they're lesbians."

"The ultimate manipulation of men," Julie said. "Do you think Millicent is a lesbian?"

"I have no way to know," I said.

"It would explain some things," Julie said.

"Can't work that way," I said. "Find the explanation and fit the circumstances to it. It's got to be the other way around."

"Well, you can keep the possibility in mind."

At the other end of the loft, Millicent, still in her shorts and tank top, dragged herself out of bed and went into the bathroom.

"I better hang up now," I said. "My guest will be wanting breakfast."

"Breakfast? It's twenty of one in the afternoon."

"She's been working nights," I said.

CHAPTER 16

"You got some coffee?" Millicent said.

"Cups in the cupboard," I said. "Coffee in the green canisters. The one with the dot on the top is decaf."

Millicent looked at the coffeemaker and the canisters and me.

"I don't know how to make coffee," she said, the way you'd explain to an idiot that you were unable to fly.

"I'll show you," I said.

"Whyn't you just make it for me," she said. "You're the one who brought me here."

"It's better if you don't have to depend on someone to make your coffee," I said. "See, the filter goes in here, then the coffee, and the water here."

She watched me, radiant with contempt, as I made the coffee.

"Next time you can make it," I said.

"Sure," she said.

While the coffee brewed, she sat on a stool at my kitchen counter and stared at nothing.

"Do you want the paper?" I said.

She shook her head.

"Would you like something to eat?" I said.

She made a face. When the coffee had brewed I poured some in a cup and handed it to her.

"You got cream and sugar?" she said.

"The sugar's right there in the bowl, the spoons are in the drawer right below where you're sitting," I said. "Milk's in the refrigerator."

She didn't move. I didn't move. Finally she got up and went to the refrigerator and got some milk. I went back to reading a book by Vincent Scully. The loft was quiet. Rosie got up from where she had been lying on my feet and went over and looked up at Millicent in case she might be going to eat something.

"Is that a dog?" Millicent said.

"That's Rosie," I said. "Rosie is a miniature bull terrier."

"Does he bite?"

"She does not," I said.

"I hate dogs," Millicent said.

"How endearing," I said.

"Huh?"

"It's fun sharing," I said.

She looked at me a little suspiciously.

"Well, I do. They don't do anything. They just hang around and eat and poop all over the place."

"Actually," I said, "that's not true. Dogs are naturally rather careful where they poop. It's why you can housebreak them."

"Well, I don't like them anyway," she said.

"Because they don't do anything useful?" I said.

"I don't know, why are you always asking me stuff? I say something and you want to talk all about it."

"And you don't," I said.

"No."

"Then why do you say it?"

"Say what?"

"Stuff you don't want to talk about?"

"I don't know."

We were quiet. She got up and went and got more coffee and brought it back and added milk and sugar and sat back on the stool. Rosie never moved from the position she had assumed at the bottom, her nose pointed straight up at Millicent, her squat body motionless. She looked like a small black-and-white pyramid.

"Isn't she cute?" I said.

"Who?"

"Rosie."

Millicent shrugged.

"What good is she?"

"I love her," I said. "She gives me something to care about."

Millicent stared at me for a while.

"That doesn't make any sense," she said, "loving something that doesn't do anything for you."

"It certainly doesn't," I said. "What size are you? Four?"

"I guess so. My mother always bought all my clothes."

"Well, I think some of my stuff will fit you. Go take a shower and then we'll pick out something."

"Why have I got to shower?" she said.

"Clean is good," I said. "Especially if you're going to be wearing my clothes."

"I don't want to take a shower."

I nodded.

"Of course you don't," I said. "And up to a point I care about what you want. But we're past the point. Either take a shower or I'll drag you in there and hold you under."

She stared at me. I stared back. Finally she shrugged and got up and walked into the bathroom.

"Shampoo your hair," I said.

The door closed. I cleaned up her coffee cup and the coffeemaker and gave Rosie a dog biscuit. Then I went and laid out several pairs of jeans and several tee shirts on my bed, so Millicent would feel like she had a choice. She came out of the bathroom with a towel wrapped around her. Her hair was straight and glistening. Her nails were clean. She didn't look anywhere near fifteen. I gestured at the clothes.

"Pick something," I said.

She took the first pair of jeans on the bed and the nearest tee shirt.

"You have any underwear?" I said.

"No."

"Of course not," I said. "Why would you."

"I won't wear yours," she said.

"That's right," I said. "We'll get you some next time we're out."

CHAPTER 17

We came back from the Chestnut Hill Mall with clothes for Millicent. Rosie was in the back-seat looking out the window and gargling at other dogs when she saw them. Millicent was up front with me.

"So where you get the money to buy these clothes?" Millicent said. "Alimony?"

"I don't get alimony."

"How come?"

"I don't want it. There's no reason he should support me the rest of my life."

"So how come you can afford to buy me clothes."

"I do detective work," I said. "People pay me. Like your parents did."

"My mother says a woman alone's got no chance."

"No more than a fish does," I said. "Without a bicycle."

"Huh?"

"Just me amusing myself," I said.

"Well, I'd take the alimony," Millicent said.

"Alimony destroys any kind of relationship people might have," I said.

"Well, you're divorced, aren't you?"

"It doesn't mean we hate each other," I said. "If there were alimony, eventually we would."

"So how come you got a divorce if you don't hate each other?"

"We're still working on that one," I said.

When we pulled up in front of my loft we found a long silver Mercedes Benz parked on the curb. Junior and Ty-Bop were outside, Junior leaning on the fender, Ty-Bop fidgeting on the sidewalk by my front door.

"Who are those colored guys?" Millicent said.

"The big one's name is Junior," I said. "The little one is Ty-Bop. The man in the car will be Tony Marcus."

"Who's he?"

"Runs the prostitution around here," I said. "He used to be your boss."

"What do they want?"

Millicent was very much less bellicose than she had been. She seemed to be getting smaller as she looked at Junior and Ty-Bop. Her shoulders hunched.

"I don't know," I said.

"They want me?"

"Tony helped me find you," I said.

"Let's drive away."

"Tony wants to talk, he'll talk," I said. "Now or later. May as well be now."

"I don't want to talk."

"You don't have to," I said. "You stay here with Rosie. I'll see what he wants."

"I don't want you to go." Millicent said.

I smiled at her.

"I'll talk with Tony. We don't want Junior to come over and bite one of the doors off."

I got out and closed the door and walked over

to the Mercedes. The back door opened and Tony Marcus stepped out, looking elegant in a pinstripe suit and a pin collar shirt. His neck was a little soft, as if he'd become so successful he didn't need to be muscular anymore.

"We need to talk, Sunny Randall," Tony said.

"Sure," I said.

Tony looked at my car.

"Got the little hooker, I see," Tony said.

"Yes."

"What's that thing in there with her?" Tony said.

"My dog, Rosie."

"That's a dog?"

"Yes."

Tony offered his arm.

"Walk along with me a little, Sunny Randall."

I took his arm and we walked slowly east in front of my building. Junior and Ty-Bop followed us.

"I wondered how quick you'd find her," Tony said.

"I know."

"And I wondered how you'd deal with my man Pharaoh, when you did find her."

"I know."

"Got to say this for you, Sunny Randall," Tony said. "You done pretty good."

"Yes," I said.

"Like to have seen it," Tony said. "You sticking a gun up Pharaoh's nose and taking one of his whores away."

Tony laughed softly. It was a surprisingly high laugh, almost a giggle.

"He told you about it?" I said.

"Hell no," Tony said. "Some of the other girls saw it. I keep track of shit."

We walked a few steps further in silence. At the end of my building Tony turned with my hand still on his arm, and we began to walk back. However his neck may have softened, his arm was strong. Ty-Bop and Junior let us pass and fell in behind us again.

"I got no problem with it," Tony said. "My pimps can't hang on to their whores, I find me somebody that can."

"I'm just helping you with quality control," I said.

"Sure you are, Sunny Randall. Problem is that somebody else looking for that little whore, too."

We walked. I waited.

"You quiet for a broad, Sunny Randall."

"And you're not," I said. "Who's looking for her."

Tony was laughing his high, soft laugh again.

"Goddamn," he said. " 'And you're not.' Goddamn. Sunny Randall, you crack me up."

"I know, sometimes I nearly overwhelm myself. Who's looking for her?"

"Some Irish guys," Tony said. "Came by to see Pharaoh, said they was looking for the little whore. We talking pop-u-larity, here. First you, then the two Irish guys."

"I'm a trendsetter," I said.

"So Pharaoh don't want to say that some pretty little blond chick come along and took

95

her away from him, so he say he don't know where she is and the two Irish guys don't believe it, so they beat up on Pharaoh till he tell them what happen."

"And?"

"And he tole them. He maybe dress it up a little so he don't look like a fucking doofus, which he is, and he don't tell them your name because he say he don't remember it. He tell them some female detective come and took his new little whore."

"Who are these guys?"

"Don't know."

"You sure they want Millicent?"

"Millicent Patton, they said."

"You know why?"

"Pharaoh didn't ask. They didn't say."

I nodded. We reached the other end of my building and Tony turned again.

"Do you believe Pharaoh?" I said.

"Junior helped me talk to him," Tony said. "Pharaoh not doing no lying to me and Junior."

"Do you think they'll ask you?" I said.

Tony shrugged.

"If they do you think you'll tell them?"

"Ain't inclined to be helpful to somebody beats up one of my pimps."

We strolled quietly again.

"Inclined maybe to let my man Junior beat up on them, truth be known."

"How is Pharaoh?" I said.

"Pharaoh's dead," he said.

"They killed him?"

Tony shook his head. I felt the truth all at once, an electric tingle in my stomach.

"You killed him," I said.

"Can't have one of my pimps giving whores away to every little blond cutie comes by with a gun," Tony said.

We reached his car. He stopped. Ty-Bop opened the door. Tony got in. Junior went around and eased in behind the driver's seat. Ty-Bop closed Tony's door and got in the front. The car started. Tony's rear window slid down silently. Tony smiled at me.

"Look sharp, Sunny Randall," he said.

The car slid away from the curb and cruised almost silently away.

CHAPTER 18

Millicent was looking at one of the cityscapes I was painting. It stood on an easel in the studio, under the skylight where I got the sun until midafternoon.

"Is that supposed to be Boston?" she said.

"It's supposed to be a painting," I said.

"Of what?"

"How Chinatown looks to me when you approach it from around Lincoln Street."

"I never been to Chinatown."

"Really? You like Chinese food?"

"I never had any."

"We'll go," I said.

"What if I don't like it?"

"Chinatown?"

"Chinese food."

"Don't eat it," I said.

"What if I'm hungry?"

"I don't plan to starve you," I said. "We'll go eat some other kind of food."

"Even if you've already paid for the Chinese stuff?"

"Yes. Sometimes six bucks doesn't mean a thing to me."

She looked at the painting some more. I hadn't told her about the Irish guys. I might have to, because she might be the only one who knew what they wanted. But right now it was like training a horse. I just wanted to gentle her down.

"How come you painted this?" she said.

"I liked the way it looked, the shape of it, the colors at that time of day."

"You mean it's not always the same color?"

"Color is a function of light," I said. "Light changes, the color changes."

"Weird," Millicent said. "You get paid for this?"

"I sell some pictures," I said.

"Will you sell this one?"

"I don't know."

"So you might be wasting your time."

"I don't think of painting as a waste of time," I said.

"Well, if you don't get paid, what good is it?"

"I like it."

"That's all?"

"I know how to do it. I like doing it."

"That's all?"

"That's all," I said.

She was quiet for a while. When we got home she had immediately gone into the bathroom and put on her new underwear. Some of which was pretty nice.

"Like the dog," Millicent said.

"The dog?"

"Yeah. You have a dog just because you want to, no good reason."

"Maybe that is a good reason," I said.

"You supposed to have a reason for stuff," Millicent said.

"Like why you ran away from home?"

"I told you, I don't like it there."

"Oh yeah," I said.

Rosie had found the long rhomboid of sunshine that slanted in through the skylight, and was lying in it on her back, with her short legs sticking straight up and her tongue lolling out of the side of her mouth.

"I'm going to have to tell your parents I found you," I said.

"You told me you wouldn't."

"No. I told you you didn't have to go home."

"You tell them and they'll make me come home," she said.

"I won't tell them where you are, but they have the right to know you're alive and well."

"They'll make you tell," Millicent said.

"No," I said.

"You work for them."

"I work for myself."

"But they're paying you."

"That's their problem."

"You won't tell them where I am?"

"No."

"Ever?"

"I don't know about ever," I said. "But I won't tell them until you and I have decided it's in your best interest."

"Even if they won't pay you anymore?"

"Even then."

The doorbell rang. Rosie was instantly on her feet in full yap. As I walked to the door I took my gun off the bureau and held it at my side. I looked through the peephole. It was Richie. When he came in Millicent was as far at the other end of the loft as she could get.

If Richie saw the gun, which he did because he saw everything, he didn't comment.

"Hello," I said.

"Hello."

There was never anything casual when we saw each other. No greeting was routine. There was a kind of charge between us that had been there since we were in elementary school and became pals, without any knowledge that my father was trying to put his father in jail. And his uncle. I had never not been glad to see him, even in the depths of it, when we couldn't stand each other and he was so possessive I thought I'd fragment. Even then I was always aware that seeing him was special, and I was always aware that it was the same for him.

Rosie was ecstatic. She jumped and wiggled and chased her tail until Richie picked her up and held her in his right arm while he rubbed her belly with his left. She managed to lap his face awkwardly while this was going on.

"Millicent," I said. "This is my ex-husband, Richie Burke. Richie, this is my friend Millicent Patton."

She stayed at the far end. Richie put Rosie down and walked the length of the loft and put his hand out.

"Hello, Millicent."

She took his hand, limply. I'd have to speak to her about that. I hate a limp handshake.

"How do you do," Millicent said with no hint of enthusiasm.

Richie walked back to the kitchen and sat at my counter.

"You called?" he said.

I put the gun back on top of the bureau.

"I did," I said. "I have to run out and talk with Millicent's parents and I wondered if you could stay with her?"

"Sure."

"Julie's working, and Spike's working and I know you work, but you're not on a time clock and... I'm babbling."

"Sure," Richie said.

"I'm not telling anyone she's here," I said.

"And you don't want anyone to come take her away," Richie said.

He spoke softly so that Millicent wouldn't overhear him. She was as far away as she could get and still be in the loft, staring out my east window at the Fort Point cityscape.

"That's right."

"Which you fear is a possibility."

"You noticed the gun," I said.

"Yeah. I'm very alert."

I told him about the Irish guys.

"That's it," Richie said. "All you know is two Irish guys?"

"That's all Tony said."

"Tony thinks all non-Africans are Irish," Richie said. "Doesn't mean it's anyone we know."

When Richie said we, it always meant his family.

"I know."

"I'll ask around, however," he said.

I nodded.

"Millicent," I said loudly enough for her to hear. "I'm going to talk with your parents."

"He going to stay here?" Millicent said.

"Yes. I'll be an hour or two."

"And you don't think I can take care of myself?"

"He's here for Rosie," I said. "Anything I should tell your parents?"

"No."

I took my gun off the bureau and put it on. Richie walked to the door with me.

"You have a gun?" I said.

He smiled at me.

"Of course you do," I said and went out.

Behind me I heard the dead bolt slide into place on the inside.

CHAPTER 19

The fire in the fireplace looked exactly the same. It would always look exactly the same. It was a gas fire. I was looking good. Double-breasted blue pinstripe suit, white shirt open at the throat. Black ankle boots. Tiny silver hoop earrings. Brock Patton was behind his desk, in his big high-backed, red leather swivel chair, where he seemed to feel most comfortable. Betty Patton sat in a caramel-colored leather wing chair to his left.

"You've found her then?" Patton said.

"Yes. She's well and safe."

"Where is she?"

"I can't tell you that."

"You what?" Betty Patton's voice was like chilled steel.

"I can't tell you where she is," I said.

"Why not," Betty said.

"She doesn't want you to know."

"Ms. Randall, are we not employing you?"

"So far," I said.

"Don't be ridiculous," Betty said. "Where is she?"

I shook my head.

"You cannot sit here and tell me you are going to substitute the judgment of a fifteen-year-old runaway for that of her parents," Betty said.

"Actually, I'm substituting my judgment," I said.

"You have no right."

"You hired me," I said. "You didn't purchase me."

"And we can fire you," Betty said. Her voice remained quiet and very cold.

"Something happened," I said. "That made her run away."

"What?"

"I don't know."

"Then how do you know something happened."

It was as if Brock had disappeared. It was me and Betty Patton.

"Woman's intuition."

"I have resources," Betty said. "Give me back my daughter or face serious consequences."

"You wouldn't have a thought, either of you, as to what might have been the, ah, precipitating event in your daughter's departure?"

"There was no event. Millicent is spoiled and childish. But she is quite capable of manipulating any adult gullible enough to believe her."

"Do you have anyone but me looking for her?"

"Perhaps we should."

"But you don't?"

"Of course not."

"She's afraid of something," I said.

"What?"

"I don't know."

Betty's ugly little laugh was derisive. "She's a neurotic child," Betty said.

"Has she been getting therapy?" I said.

"Doesn't every teenaged brat that can't cut it get therapy?" Brock said.

When he spoke it felt like an intrusion, something foreign to the angry exclusivity that connected me to Betty.

"Shut up, Brock," Betty said.

"Isn't that sweet," Brock said. " 'Shut up,' she explained."

"Who's her therapist?" I said.

"That is no concern of yours," Betty said.

I nodded.

"Did you or your husband have a fight with Millicent before she left?"

"Ms. Randall," Betty said. "I am not some Irish scrub woman, I do not fight with my daughter."

"She's very angry with you," I said.

"Millicent doesn't know what she's angry about," Betty said. "She is a petulant adolescent. Had you ever raised one you might be less inclined to take her at face value."

Actually I thought it was Betty that was taking Millicent at face value.

"Perhaps," I said.

"Do you have a license to do what you do?" Betty asked.

"Yes."

"Well, if my daughter is not back here promptly you will lose it."

"Oh, oh!" I said.

"And that will be the least unpleasant thing you'll face."

"If you're going to threaten me," I said, "you need to be specific."

Betty shook her head. I looked at Brock. "And you?"

Brock tossed his hands in the air.

"I have long ago given up trying to work things out with women."

I sat for a moment.

"Okay," I said. "Your daughter is well and safe. And, despite the paralyzing impact of your threat, I will make every attempt to keep her that way."

I stood. Neither of them moved.

"I have warned you, Ms. Randall," Betty said, "don't take what I've said lightly."

"Hard not to," I said, and turned and marched out.

I love a good exit line.

CHAPTER 20

Rosie and Millicent were with Richie. I didn't know where. And I was sitting at a table for four with Spike, watching the new cabaret act he had put together for the restaurant.

"It's funny," I said to Spike. "I can't live with Richie, but I trust him even with Rosie."

Spike was watching the show too intently to do anything more than nod. I didn't mind: the remark had been as much to me as it had been to him, anyway. While I was thinking about my remark, and Spike was thinking about his cabaret, Don Bradley came in and sat at the table with us. The cabaret singers started a medley of World War II songs.

"Hi, Sunny," he said. "I been trying to reach you."

"I know."

"...praise the Lord and pass the ammunition..."

"I guess I got a little buzzed at the end of it, I don't remember the way we parted, exactly."

"I do."

"I didn't get out of hand, I hope," he grinned at me. "Sometimes I get a little wild."

"Don, please," I said. "I'm afraid we're not really meant for each other. Let's let it go."

"Damn it, Sunny, I thought we were having a good time."

Don raised his voice a little. It was enough to break Spike's concentration on the cabaret. Which I knew Spike didn't like. He looked at Don.

"Don," I said. "You spent the evening talking about yourself until you got so drunk I had to half carry you into your home, at which time you tried to force yourself on me."

"That's not how it seemed to me, Sunny."

Spike had half turned now, and leaned his elbow on the table and his chin on his elbow and had his face very close to Don's, listening intently. When I spoke Spike's eyes shifted to me, but his face stayed close to Don's.

"I don't wish to argue it," I said. "I'd simply prefer not to go out with you."

"I'm not taking no for an answer," Don said.

Spike's closeness was beginning to make him uncomfortable. He looked at Spike.

"...with anyone else but me, anyone else but me..."

"Excuse me?" he said.

"Certainly," Spike said.

"I mean, excuse me, why are you interfering with our conversation?"

"I do that, sometimes," Spike said.

"Well, I don't like it," Don said.

There was an edge to his voice. He was not a man to be crossed.

"Gay bashing," Spike said.

"What?"

"I'm a charming gay man, and you have turned on me for no discernible reason. I say it's gay bashing."

"I didn't even know you were gay."

"For crissake," Spike said. "What am I supposed to do, sit in your lap?"

"Of course not."

"This is blatant homophobia," Spike said. "Sunny?"

I smiled and didn't answer.

"...a hubba hubba hubba, hello, Jack..."

"See," Spike said.

Don said. "Why don't you just butt out."

"Sunny has made it clear that she doesn't like you and doesn't want to go out with you," Spike said. "I felt it was important that you know I feel the same way."

"What?"

"Stay away from Sunny," Spike said.

And then Spike did what he does. I don't know how he does it. Something happens behind his eyes, and whatever it is shows through, and quite suddenly there's nothing playful about Spike.

Don saw it and it scared him.

"You're threatening me," he said finally.

"You bet," Spike said. "Think how embarrassing it'll be, to tell the guys at the health club that you got your clock cleaned by a ho-mo-sex-ual."

Don didn't move. Better men than Don had been frightened by Spike. But he didn't want to back down in front of me.

"...remember Pearl Harbor, as we march against the foe..."

"Don," I said. "There's nothing between you and me."

"I'm not scared of him," Don said.

"You should be," I said. "Walk away from this. There's nothing here for you."

Don sat for another moment. Then he stood up.

"All right, but only because you asked me, Sunny."

"Sure," I said. "I understand. Sorry it didn't work out."

Don nodded and said, "Good-bye, Sunny."

"Good-bye, Don."

To salvage his self-regard he gave Spike a hard look. Spike smiled at him. Don turned away and walked stiffly out of the restaurant.

"I could have chased him away myself," I said to Spike.

"Sure," Spike said, "but it's like the old joke, praise God you didn't have to."

It was after six and I was starting supper for Millicent and me. She had slept much of the afternoon and now sat at the kitchen counter drinking a Coke and watching me. I had a cookbook open on the counter beside me. I had put a carving knife across it to keep the pages from flipping over. Rosie was between and around my ankles as I worked.

"You like to cook?" I said to Millicent.

"No."

"Do you know how?"

"No."

"Would you like to learn?"

"You a good cook?" Millicent said.

"No. But I'm getting better. Actually I'm learning, too. I'd love somebody to learn with me."

"Who's teaching you?"

"I've been watching Martha Stewart," I said.

"Who?"

"A woman on television," I said.

"What's in the plastic bag?"

"Pizza dough," I said. "I buy it at a place in the North End and let it warm a little and then roll it out."

"You're making pizza?"

"Yes, white, with vinegar peppers and caramelized onions."

"Whaddya mean, white?"

"No tomato sauce."

"What's that other stuff—whatchamacallit onions and peppers."

"Sweet and sour," I said. "Here, roll out some of this pizza dough."

"I don't know how to do that."

"Take this roller," I said. "Put some flour on this board."

I showed her.

"Put a little more flour on top of the dough."

I showed her again.

"Roll it from the center out."

Millicent sighed a large sigh and took the rolling pin. She dabbed at the dough with it.

"No, no," I said. "Roll it."

I took the pin and showed her. The dough sat there inertly. When I rolled it in one direction it shrank up in another. I rolled more vigorously. The dough sat there more inertly. After five hard minutes I had a lump of pizza dough the same size and thickness with which I had started. I put the rolling pin down and stepped back and looked at the dough.

"You ever make this before?" Millicent said.

"Not exactly," I said.

"Maybe if you just squished it with your hands," she said.

I tried it. The dough was recalcitrant. I picked it up and dropped it into the trash compactor. Then I took the dish of sliced onions and chopped up peppers and scraped them into the trash.

"If at first you don't succeed," I said, "have something else for supper."

Millicent made a little sound that might almost have been a snicker.

"You don't know how to cook for shit," Millicent said.

"I'm learning," I said. "I'm learning."

She made the sound again.

"You were pounding and shoving that sucker and it wasn't doing a thing," Millicent said.

I laughed. She might have laughed. We might have been laughing together.

"The perversity of inanimate objects," I said.

"Huh?"

"It's something my father always says."

"Oh. So what are we going to eat?"

"What do you like?" I said.

"I like peanut butter."

"Me, too," I said. "And even better, I think I can make a sandwich."

"For crissake, Sunny, I can make a peanut butter sandwich."

"With jelly?"

"Sure."

"Oh, yeah? Okay, smarty pants, go ahead. Show me."

After supper we took Rosie for a walk along

Congress Street down toward the Fort Point Channel.

"So can you cook anything?" Millicent said.

"Some things." I said. "Who knew pizza dough was going to be ugly?"

"How come you're not a good cook?"

"Probably the same reason you're not," I said. "Nobody taught me."

"My mother's a good cook," Millicent said. "She teach you?"

"No. She said I would mess up her kitchen."

"My mother's kitchen was always a mess," I said. "Her problem was she didn't know how to cook either."

"I don't see why a woman has to cook." Millicent said.

"Nobody has to cook," I said. "Only if they want to."

Rosie had found a crushed earthworm on the edge of the sidewalk and was rolling purposefully on it.

"What's she doing?"

"Rolling on a dead worm," I said.

"Gross," Millicent said, "why don't you make her stop?"

"She seems to like it," I said.

"Why's she doing it?"

"I have no idea," I said.

Rosie stopped rolling and stood up and sniffed at the worm remains, and then looked proudly up at me and stepped out along the sidewalk.

"How come you're trying to learn to cook?" Millicent said.

"I like to make things," I said. "And I like to eat."

Millicent shrugged. Rosie charged ahead on her leash as if she had a place to go and was in a rush to get there. At Sleeper Street, downtown Boston loomed up solidly ahead of us. To the right was the Children's Museum with the big wooden milk bottle, and the tea party ship replica bobbed on the water next to the Congress Street Bridge.

"I suppose," I said, "as I think of it, that I also probably think at some level or other that the more I can do for myself, the less dependent I will be on anyone else."

"I think it's easier just to let somebody else do it," Millicent said. "Then you don't have to do anything."

"Which is why you're here," I said, "walking around South Boston with a detective you barely know."

Millicent was silent. Rosie was adamant, as she always was, about looking at the water under the bridge. We stopped on the beginning of it while she stared over the edge, her wedge-shaped head jammed through the bridge railing. The water was dirty. I looked up at Millicent. She was crying. Hallelujah! An emotion! I put my arm around her. She was thin and stiff.

"On the other hand, you'll know me really well in a while. And when you do you'll absolutely love me."

She didn't say anything. She stood rigidly with the tears running down her cheeks, then the rigidity went away, and she turned in against my shoulder and cried as hard as she could while I patted her and Rosie gazed intently down at the black water.

22

Well into midmorning Millicent was still asleep. Rosie had hopped up on the bed and was sleeping next to her in the crook of her bent legs. I was still in my silk robe, at my easel, drinking some coffee and trying to get the right yellow onto the restaurant sign in my Chinatown painting, when the doorbell rang. I went and buzzed the speaker downstairs.

"Package for Sunny Randall," the voice said.

"Who from?" I said.

"I don't know, lady, I just drive the truck."

"Okay," I said. "Second floor."

I buzzed the downstairs door open and stood looking out the peephole in my door. In a moment the big old elevator eased to a stop and the doors, originally designed for freight, slid open. There were two men with a large cardboard box. They carried it as if it was empty. I opened the broom closet next to the door and took out a short double-barreled shotgun that my father had confiscated from a dope dealer and passed on to me. I cocked both barrels and as I walked back to the door, my bell rang. Rosie jumped down from the bed and hustled to the door in case it might be Richie. I looked through the peephole again. The box had been pushed aside and the two men stood waiting. I opened the door a foot and stepped away, keeping it between me and them. Rosie sniffed and wagged and milled around their feet as they shoved the door open and came in. The first man shoved her out of the way with his foot. The second guy came through right behind his buddy, his hand under his pea coat. I wasn't dressed for company. I had the shotgun at my shoulder, and I could feel the butt of it through the thin silk of my robe.

"Freeze," I said.

The guy with the pea coat said, "Shit," and brought his hand out with a nine in it. I fired one barrel. It was a 10-gauge gun loaded with fours and it took him full in the chest at two feet. He went backwards into the hall and fell on his back. My ears were ringing. In the enclosed area the sound of the gunshot was painful. The second man threw his hands up as I turned the gun toward him.

"No," he said. "No, no, no."

"Flat on your goddamned face," I said, "now. Hands behind your neck. Right-fucking-now."

The second man went down. I held the shotgun against the back of his head while I patted him down. I took a .357 Mag from his hip. Then I backed four steps to the kitchen counter, put the .357 down and dialed 911. I kept the shotgun level and aimed over the crook of my arm. The second man remained motionless, his hands clasped behind his head, his face on the floor. Beyond him in the entryway his partner lay silently on his back, with one leg twitching occasionally.

"There's been a shooting," I said, and gave my name and address. "Second floor, there's a man down."

I hung up and glanced over toward the bedroom end of the loft. Rosie had disappeared, I suspected under the bed. Millicent was out of sight, too, maybe sharing space with Rose.

"Millicent," I said. "It's okay. The police are on the way."

No one spoke.

"Is Rosie there with you?" I said.

A voice said, "Yes."

"The cops will be here soon," I said.

I walked back to the second man, face-down on the floor.

"You want to tell me what this is about?" I said.

"Don't know."

I prodded his right temple with the shotgun.

"You kicked my dog," I said. "I might shoot you for that."

"I just pushed her," he said. "I didn't want to step on her."

"Why are you here?"

117

"I don't know. Honest to God. I just come with Terry. He said we was going to pick up some girl."

"Why?"

"Don't know."

I prodded again.

"Swear on my mother," he said. "Terry just says it'll be some easy dough. Just a couple broads."

"Terry the guy in the hall?" I said.

"Yeah."

"What's his last name?"

"Nee."

"What's your name."

"Mike."

Outside on Summer Street I could hear the first siren.

"Can you give me a break," Mike said.

"Who sent you?" I said.

"I don't know. I just come along pick up a day's pay from Terry."

"Did you rough up a pimp named Pharaoh Fox?" I said.

"Don't know his name, me and Terry slapped a black guy around a little. He was a pimp."

"Why?"

"Something about a girl."

"Do you know the girl's name?"

"No. Terry did."

The siren dwindled and went silent in front of my loft. Then another one.

"You gonna gimme a break?"

"No," I said. "I'm not."

Mike didn't say anything and in another minute the elevator door opened and two cops walked out, service pistols in hand, held against the leg, the barrel pointing at the ground. Behind them came two EMTs. I let the shotgun hang by my side. I was holding my robe together with my left hand. The older of the two cops put out his hand, and I gave him the gun. I was glad to give it up. Then I could hold my robe together with both hands. The younger cop stood over Mike and patted him down. One of the EMTs went down on the floor beside Terry Nee.

"He's cooked," the EMT said.

"There's a gun on the counter," I said. "I took it from Mike on the floor."

"Glock on the floor out there," the younger cop said.

"Leave everything for the detectives," the older cop said. "You, on the floor, you stay right there."

The young cop left Mike and went and bent over and looked at the dead man.

"Well, hello," he said. "It's Terry Nee."

"If it had to be somebody," the older cop said, his eyes moving around the room as he spoke, "it might just as well be Terry Nee."

The young cop opened the big cardboard box and peered in.

"Empty," he said.

Rosie crept out from under the bed waggling tentatively. I scooched down and put my arms out and she scuttled over, and I picked her up. Millicent stood up behind the bed and stayed there, her back against the wall. The older cop looked at Rosie who was lapping my neck as if it were her last chance.

"Not an attack dog, I'd guess."

"Not unless you're a liver snap," I said.

He looked at a scrap of paper.

"Sonya Randall?"

"Sunny," I said.

"Sunny Randall?"

"Yes."

"You Phil Randall's kid?"

"Yes."

"I was in a cruiser once with Phil. You're a lot better-looking."

"Yes," I said.

"You want to tell me what happened?"

I could hear more sirens on Summer Street. And the sound of the elevator heading up. It was going to be a long day.

CHAPTER

23

It helped that I had been a cop. It helped that I was a licensed private investigator. It helped that I had a gun permit. It helped that Millicent confirmed my story, however monosyllabically. It helped that I was a woman defending a young girl against two known thugs. It helped that I was kind of cute. It probably helped a little that Rosie was cuter than is legally permissible in many states. And it helped a lot that I was Phil Randall's daughter. We didn't have to go downtown. We agreed that Millicent would be better off if she weren't mentioned to the press. The lead detective on the case was a sergeant named Brian Kelly who had thick black hair and a cute butt and a wonderful smile.

"We'll need to talk again, Sunny," he said about five in the afternoon as they were cleaning up the crime scene. "Is it okay if I call you Sunny?"

"Absolutely, Sergeant," I said.

"And I'd appreciate you calling me Brian," he said.

We were sitting at my kitchen table with Rosie plomped on one of Brian's feet, looking up at him with her tongue lolling out. Millicent was sitting up on my bed with her knees to her chin and her arms wrapped around them, staring at the television.

"I'll do what I can to shelter the kid. If there's a trial she may have to testify, but I doubt that there'll be a trial."

"You don't plan to bring old Mike into court?"

"The guy you didn't shoot?" Brian looked at his notes. "Mike Leary. Don't know him. But he hangs around with Terry Nee, we'll find some use for him, and he'll plea-bargain."

"Fine," I said.

"You don't have any thoughts you've not shared with me, do you, about why they were here and what they were doing?"

121

"You know what I know," I said.

"Maybe," Brian said.

"Would I lie to you?"

Brian smiled at me. When he smiled his eyes widened a little and seemed to get brighter.

"Of course you would, Sunny. We both know that."

"So young and yet so cynical," I said.

He stood and put his notebook away. I stood with him.

"Lemme get back to the station," Brian said, "and sort of fold this up and put it away for the night. I'll call you in a couple days."

"Fine."

"You okay?"

"Sure," I said. "I'm fine."

"You ever kill somebody before?"

"No."

"It's sort of a heavy thing," he said.

"I know," I said. "I'll be fine."

"I'll leave a cruiser out front for the night, just until we shake this down a little."

"Thank you."

"Okay. I'll call you."

"Do," I said.

And he left. I followed him to the door and locked it after he left. Rosie went down the length of the loft and jumped up on the bed beside Millicent and lay down. I sat at my kitchen counter for a while. My ears were still ringing. When the mass of buckshot had hit him, Terry Nee's shirt had disappeared in a mass of blood. I wondered if he felt it. He might have made a sound when he went backward. I wondered if he had been alive when his leg was twitching, or if it was just some weird reflex and Terry was already somewhere else. I'd have to clean the shotgun. If you fired them and didn't clean them, the barrel got pitted. Terry was a guy who couldn't believe a woman would shoot him, or couldn't allow himself to back down to a woman. Whatever it was, it killed him.

They would have taken the girl. He went for his gun. He'd have shot me. With a 10-gauge shotgun at two feet you can't aim to wound. I had to kill him. The ringing wouldn't go away. I shook my head a little and got up and went to the cabinet and got a green bottle of Glenfiddich and a short glass. I poured an inch of scotch and sipped it, and poured some more. I could feel my heart moving in my chest. I was aware of my breathing. It seemed shallow. I took another sip of scotch, and shivered slightly and got up and went to the refrigerator and added some ice. As I was putting the ice in, some of it slipped from my hand and scattered on the floor. When I bent to pick it up I dropped the glass. The glass broke. I couldn't leave broken glass on the floor with Rosie in the house, so I went to the broom closet and got the dustpan and a broom and cleaned up the glass and ice, and put it in the trash compactor and closed the compactor and turned the switch. I walked over to the broom closet and put the broom away and hung the dustpan on the hook. It slipped off the hook and dropped to the floor. I bent to pick it up and felt all the strength go from me, and sat down on the floor and began to cry. I heard Rosie jump down from the bed and trot down the length of the loft. She came around the kitchen counter and began to lap my face. Maybe to comfort me. Maybe because she liked salt. Then Millicent appeared around the corner of the counter, barefooted, and stared at me. Her face was stark and colorless. Her eyes seemed nearly black in the oval of her face.

"You all right?" she said.

Rosie lapped industriously. I nodded.

"How come you're crying?" Millicent said.

Her voice had the flat tinny sound fear makes.

I shook my head. She stood. I sat. Then I put my hand up and took hers and squeezed it. Rosie lapped the other cheek. I could feel control starting to come back. I was beginning to breathe more slowly. I let go of Millicent's hand and put Rosie off my lap and got to my feet. I got another glass and put some ice in it and poured some single malt into it.

"Can I have some?" Millicent said.

I got her a glass and handed it to her. She added ice and poured some scotch over it. We sat together at the counter. We both took a drink. Millicent frowned.

"What is that stuff?"

"Single malt scotch," I said.

"It's not like any scotch I ever had."

I nodded. We were quiet. Rosie lay on the rug sideways to us, looking at us obliquely.

"It bother you, shooting that guy?" Millicent said.

"Not at the time," I said. "Now it does."

She shrugged and stared at the scotch for a bit and took another small sip.

"What'd they want?" she said.

I took in a deep breath and let it out slowly.

"You," I said.

Her eyes got bigger.

"My mother sent them," she said.

"I don't know who sent them," I said.

"My mother."

The way she said "mother" was chilling. If I ever had children, and the clock was starting to tick on me, I prayed that they would never call me mother in that voice.

"How would your mother know men like that?" I said.

Millicent looked at my counter and didn't answer. I waited. Millicent sipped some more of the scotch. She was five or six years below the minimum age. I was contributing to the delinquency of a minor. So what? Everybody else had.

"How would she?" I said.

"My mom knows a lot of men," Millicent said, still staring down at the countertop.

"And you think she would send them here with guns to get you?"

"Sure."

"These same two men beat up Pharaoh Fox, looking for you."

Millicent shrugged.

"You think your mother sent them to do that, too?"

"Sure."

"The man I... the dead man was a known criminal. The police knew him. He was a strong-arm man, an enforcer."

Millicent took another swallow of scotch.

"She knows guys like that," Millicent said without lifting her stare from the countertop.

I sipped my scotch. Millicent sipped hers. The room was quiet, except for the television murmuring in front of the bed at the other end of the loft.

"Millicent," I said finally. "There's more to this than that. Your mother is an affluent suburban housewife married to a very successful man. How in the hell would she come to know people like Terry Nee?"

Millicent stared at my counter some more.

"And why would she send such a person looking for you?"

Stare.

"Does this have something to do with why you ran away?"

Shrug.

I reached over and took hold of her chin with my right hand and turned her face toward me.

"Goddamn it," I said. "I just shot a man to protect you."

"And yourself," she mumbled.

"And Rosie," I said. "And I'm in this because of you. And I want to know what exactly the fuck is going on."

Tears welled suddenly. She tried to shake her head. I held on to her chin.

"What?" I said.

The tears were running down her face now. "What?"

Her breath was coming in little gasps. "What?"

"I... I saw... I saw something," she gasped.

CHAPTER 24

I got up from the counter and took my scotch with me and walked to the front window. I looked down through it at the police cruiser parked out front. It was comforting. I kept looking down at it.

"What did you see, Millicent?" I said.

Behind me was silence. I stared down at the cruiser. The silence continued. I waited. Finally she spoke.

"My mother told a man to kill somebody."

I closed my eyes. Jesus Christ. What should I say to her? I stared out the window. There was no comfort for this in the police cruiser. I had to do something. Finally, I turned back. She was sitting now, swiveled toward me on the barstool, still looking down. But now she was looking at Rosie. And her shoulders were heaving. I walked back and put my scotch down on the counter and put both my arms around her. She was stiff but she didn't struggle.

"We seem to be crying by turn," I said. "Now being your turn."

She didn't answer. She was crying spasmodically.

"This is awful," I said. "And it's probably going to get awfuller. But we're in it and we're in it together and we're going to have to get out of it together. And the only way is to talk, you and me, until we know what to do."

She cried. I held.

"Take your time," I said. "Tell me in any way you want to. No hurry. When you get calmed down. I have to know what the problem is before I can solve it."

As I held on to her I could feel her fighting for control. Rosie squeezed between our feet wanting to get in on the hug. I rubbed her belly with my toe. Millicent took in some deep breaths and then she started talking. The sound was muffled because she kept her face half pressed against my shoulder.

She told me that Betty Patton had a suite of her own on the first floor, bedroom, study, private bath, and shower off of it. Millicent was never allowed in there. She was never to use the private bathroom. She was too messy. The bathroom was for guests. Millicent of course took every opportunity to sneak into the off-limits suite and snoop about. It was how she had found the sexual pictures of her mother. And, of course, she used the bathroom as often as possible while she was in there. On the day in question, she was in the off-limits bathroom, and just coming out when the door to the study opened. Millicent ducked back and stepped into the clear glass shower stall to hide. She could hear her mother talking to a man whose voice she didn't recognize. It was a deep voice and he spoke with sort of a low rolling purr that sounded like some kind of big machine in good working order. There was strain in her mother's voice. She'd never heard her mother's voice sound like that.

"I don't care what tingles your gonads," the man purred. "But when it spills over into our business, I care."

"It won't spill over," Mother said.

"It already has," he said.

"We can prevent it from spilling anymore."

"You got a suggestion?"

"You have resources," Mother said.

"What kind of resources are we talking?"

"He'll have to be killed," Mother said. "We are too close to what we want to let this stop us."

"Brock know anything about this guy?"

"Brock doesn't know anything about anything," Mother said. "Except shooting skeet and making money."

"Okay," the man said, his soft voice filling the room with energy, "we'll clip him."

"Quickly," mother said. "Before he damages the project."

"Sure," the man said. "May I use your bathroom?"

"Of course."

The man walked into the bathroom. Millicent was pressed against the back wall of the shower, looking at him through the glass shower door. He looked back at her. Without a word, still looking at her he reached back and closed the bathroom door, and then he turned and raised the toilet seat and used the toilet and flushed and closed the toilet seat carefully. He was a medium-tall man with a thick body and very thick hands. His hair was silvery and short and brushed back. He wore a dark suit with a white shirt and a maroon silk tie. Gold cufflinks flashed beneath the sleeves of his jacket. He wore an important-looking diamond ring on the little finger of his left hand. He bent over the sink and washed his hands thoroughly and dried them on the towel that hung on the hook beside the shower. He stared at her some more while he did this, and then, without a word, he turned and walked out of the bathroom.

"One other thing," he said to Mother. "You can spread your legs for anybody you want. We don't care. You can fuck as weird as you want. We don't care. Long as it's private. You understand?"

"Of course. It was a mistake. We can correct it. It won't happen again."

"We will correct it," the man said.

Millicent heard the two of them walk across the room and open the door to the hall. The door closed. The room was silent. She stood in the shower stall in the bathroom, stiff with terror. Nothing moved in the room. She forced herself to step rigidly out of the shower stall and look around the corner of the bathroom door. The study was empty. She ran to the door, feeling as if her legs wouldn't work right, and opened it a crack and peeked into the hall. No one was there. She stepped into the hall and walked to the French doors at the end of the hall that led to the back lawn. No one stopped her. She opened the French doors and closed them soundlessly behind her and began to run.

"Why didn't he say anything to my mother," Millicent said.

"My guess is he decided he'd have to get rid of you, too, and didn't want your mother to know."

"Get rid of?"

"Kill," I said.

"Oh my God," Millicent said.

"It's okay," I said. "I won't let him."

"How are you going to stop him, you should have seen him, what he looked like, what he sounded like, you're a girl like me, for crissake, what are you going to do?"

"What have I done so far," I said.

She thought about that.

"It would be nice," I said. "If I weighed two hundred pounds and used to be a boxer. But I'm not, so we find other ways. I can shoot. I can think. I am very quick. The dangerous stuff almost always boils down to people with guns, and guns make size and strength irrelevant. With guns it only matters how tough you are, and I'm as tough as anybody they're likely to send."

She thought about that, too. She wanted to believe it, because it would make her feel safer. In principle I believed it. It was the theory under which I worked. Though I knew privately that it was a more comfortable theory when Richie was around.

"You know this man's name?" I said.

"No. You think he sent those men today?"

"Yes."

"What are we going to do?"

"We'll move tomorrow. We're all right tonight with the cops outside."

"Where we going to go?"

"Someplace safe," I said. "Do you know what deal your mother was talking about with the man?"

"No."

"Do you know who they were talking about killing?"

"Some guy who must have been bopping my mom."

"But you don't know who?"

"No."

"Sounds like somebody planning to go public with details," I said.

"Yes."

"Embarrassing, maybe," I said, "but would she have him killed for that? I mean there's a lot of that going around."

Millicent shrugged and drank some scotch. She made a face, every time, as if she were taking medicine. But it didn't cause her to stop.

"In those sex pictures you found. Was the man recognizable?"

"I think so. I didn't like looking at them."

"I don't blame you," I said. "Do you have any of those pictures?"

"No, when I ran I didn't have anything but what I was wearing."

"Are there any in your room?"

132

"No. My mother used to search my room all the time. I never dared have anything there."

"You don't know any of the men your mother has been with?"

"No."

We communed with our scotch for a moment.

"She searched your room?" I said.

"Yes. To make sure I didn't have drugs, or condoms or cigarettes, stuff like that. She said it was her responsibility to know."

I nodded.

"If she gave you enough time, I imagine you'd have fulfilled her expectations," I said.

"What's that mean?"

I shrugged.

"Just a little pop psych," I said. "Pay no attention."

CHAPTER 25

Spike had a town house with guest space on the second floor, in the South End on Warren Ave.

"I thought you lived in the South End," Millicent said to me when we were surveying the two rooms and a bath that Spike was offering.

"I live in South Boston," I said. "This is the South End. Two different places."

There was a bay window in my bedroom with a window seat. Rosie immediately commandeered it so that she could look down at Warren Avenue and bark at anything that moved.

"You're sure nobody saw us come here?" Millicent said.

I noticed that she hovered near the inner walls of the room, staying away from the windows. Her bedroom was across the hall from mine, but she stayed with me. Since the shooting she had not let me out of her sight.

"I'm not an amateur," I said. "No one followed us."

Spike came up the stairs with my suitcase and a duffel bag.

"What the hell is in here?" Spike said. "Hand grenades?"

"My face is in the suitcase," I said. "Duffel bag goes next door."

Spike dropped the suitcase.

"Come on, Millicent," he said. "I'll show you your room."

Millicent hesitated and then followed him across the hall. She looked back as she left the room.

"I'm right here," I said. "Door open."

Spike came back in a moment without her.

"You know what you're getting into," I said.

"Sure," Spike said. "You're going to the mattresses."

"I hope not. I hope we are hiding successfully."

Spike was wearing jeans and a tee shirt with a plaid flannel shirt open over the tee shirt.

When he sat on the bed I could see that he had an Army-issue Colt .45 stuck in his belt. I took some clothes out of the suitcase and put them in the top drawer of the bureau.

"Kid's scared," Spike said.

"Of course she is, there are people after her. She saw me kill one of them."

"Better than seeing you not kill him."

"True. I have to tell Richie where I am," I said.

"Sure," Spike said.

"I've got to be able to leave her here and go and find out who her mother was going to have killed, and who the people are who are trying to get her."

"Be the same people, wouldn't it," Spike said.

"That's my assumption," I said. "We can't leave Millicent alone."

"I know."

"I hate to ask, but I don't know who else. I can't ask Julie. It's too dangerous and she's got children of her own."

"I'll sit her," Spike said. "But I have to work now and then, though not very hard. Maybe you can get Richie to take a turn."

"I don't..."

"You don't want to ask him for anything," Spike said, "I know. But you don't have that luxury."

"I've already asked him a couple of times," I said.

Millicent came out of her room and across the hall and stood inside the doorway and didn't say anything. Rosie began to gargle and yap and

135

growl and bark and jump straight up and down on all four feet in the bay window. Millicent seemed to press herself into the wall by the door. Spike and I both looked out the window. There was a Yorkshire terrier being walked.

"Rat on a rope," Spike said.

"What?" Millicent said.

"Just a dog," I said. "Rosie barks at all children, and most dogs. You might as well get used to it."

"You want some lunch?" Spike said.

"Like what?" Millicent said.

"Like chicken piccata, or a lobster club sandwich?"

"What?"

"Come down with me," Spike said. "You can order what you want."

"You can cook stuff like that?"

"I'm gay, of course I can cook stuff like that."

"I didn't know you were gay."

"Yes, makes me immune to your seductive ways."

"I never met anyone gay before."

"You did," Spike said, "you just didn't know it."

Millicent looked uneasy. I didn't know if it was because she was leaving me, or because she was going with a homosexual man.

"Come on, Mill," Spike said. "You've fallen upon good times here. Make the most of it. The best thing Sunny can do with a pot is put it away."

"Go ahead," I said. "Maybe he'll give you a cooking lesson."

Millicent looked doubtfully at Spike but she went with him. Rosie, hearing talk of food, plomped down from the window seat and followed them. I went and sat on the bed and called Richie.

CHAPTER 26

I was in District 6 Station House, Area C, on Broadway, talking with Brian Kelly at his desk in the detectives' room. It was a state-of-the-art squad room, which is to say over-crowded, cluttered, and painted an ugly color. In the midst of it Brian was neat and crisp, clean-shaven and smelling of good cologne.

"Everybody agrees it's a clear case of self-defense. Nobody wants to bring charges," Brian said.

"And one of them shoved my dog with his foot."

"He got what he deserved," Brian said. "You clean that shotgun?"

"Yes."

"You don't clean them, you know, the barrel pits."

"I know."

"Ten-gauge?" he said.

"You weigh 115," I said, "you like fire-power."

Brian's teeth were even and very white,

137

and his eyes were very blue. His hands were strong-looking. He had on a white shirt with a buttoned-down collar and a black knit tie and a Harris tweed jacket. He nodded.

"You weigh 115. I'm surprised the recoil didn't put you on your ass."

"I'm very grounded," I said.

Brian smiled.

"Terry Nee was mostly a part of Bucko Meehan's crew," Brian said.

"What's Bucko's line?" I said.

"Truck hijacking, some dope dealing, extortion."

"Tell me about the extortion."

"Mostly small business owners—taverns, sub shops, liquor stores. Pay off or we'll bust up your store, or your customers, or you. Terry Nee was the bust-up specialist."

"Not a major player," I said.

"Bucko? Hell no. Worked the fringes."

"Did Terry ever freelance?"

"Sure. In Boston organized crime is an oxymoron. There are affiliations, but they're loose ones, usually ethnic. The micks hang with micks, the guineas with guineas. But everybody freelances."

"So it didn't have to be Bucko Meehan that sent Terry Nee and Mike whatsis to my house."

"No."

"What's Mike say?"

"He says he doesn't know anything. Terry asked him to go along and hold a gun. He says they were supposed to take some girl out of there. Says he didn't even know your name."

"You believe him?" I said.

"I can't turn him. We got him on attempted murder. I tell him if he'll give us who sent him he can get a lot lighter charge."

"And he stays with his story," I said.

"Un huh."

"Which means either it's true, or whoever sent them is too scary to turn on."

"Yep."

"You have any theories?"

"I'm inclined to think he's telling us everything he knows. He's looking at serious time. I think he'd rat out Al Capone if it got him a deal."

"You talked with Bucko Meehan yet?"

"Not yet, want to go with me?"

I looked at my watch. Ten-thirty. I had to be home by four, when Spike went to work.

"Sure," I said.

We talked with Bucko Meehan at the far end of the counter in a Dunkin' Donut shop across from Assembly Square in Somerville.

"Boston cremes," Bucko said. "The best."

I looked at the chocolate-covered things Bucko had in front of him and decided on a plain donut and a coffee. Brian just had coffee.

"You're missing out," Bucko said.

"I'm used to it," Brian said. "Bucko Meehan, Sunny Randall."

"How ya doin'?" Bucko said.

"Fine."

Bucko was a fat muscleman. Hard fat, my father used to call it. He was obviously strong, but his neck disappeared into several chins. He was wearing a Patriots jacket over a gray sweatshirt. The sweatshirt gapped at the waist and his belly spilled out through the gap. The donut shop was empty, except for us and a couple of people at the take-out counter. A middle-aged Hispanic woman was taking their order.

"Whaddya need from me today, Brian?"

"Couple guys that hang with you got in some trouble," Brian said.

"Who's 'at?"

"Terry Nee and Mike Leary."

Bucko shrugged. The shrug didn't say he knew them. It didn't say he didn't. People who'd spent a lifetime talking to cops learned, if they weren't stupid, to find out what the cop knew before they admitted anything.

"What kinda trouble," he said.

"Attempted murder."

"Don't know nothing about it," Bucko said.

He broke one of his donuts in two. It had a creamy filling. He took a bite, and wiped his mouth with a napkin.

"I thought Terry was part of your crew," Brian said.

"I got no crew."

"You know Terry?" I said.

"See him around," Bucko said.

"How about Mike Leary?"

"Don't know him," Bucko said.

"Terry run with anybody but you?" Brian said.

"Hell, Brian, I don't know. Terry's a good guy. He's got a lot of friends."

"He tried to break into a home in Fort Point," Brian said. "And the homeowner shot him."

"Terry?"

"Un huh."

"He dead?"

"Un huh."

"Terry's a tough guy."

"Not anymore," I said.

"Who shot him?"

"Doesn't matter," Brian said.

"Housebreak?"

"He was there for a purpose." I said. "If you didn't send him there, maybe you can speculate who did."

"Speculate? Jesus Christ, Sunny, I'm too fucking stupid to fucking speculate. What's the other guy say?"

"Says you sent them," Brian said.

"That lying sack of shit," Bucko said. "I don't even know the guy. I got nothing to do with anything in Fort Point, for crissake. I don't get east of Lechmere Square."

"Maybe doing somebody a favor?" Brian said.

"I don't know a fucking thing about it, Brian. Swear on my mother. Terry's over in Fort Point doing a B & E, I got nothing to do with it I don't care what lies some guy is telling you?"

"Why would he lie?" I said.

"He's trying to deal," Bucko said. "You know the fucking game, Sunny. He'll say whatever you want to hear."

"And maybe he'll say it in court about you, Bucko."

Bucko spread his arms palms up.

"What can I tell you. I got nothing to do with whatever Terry and this other jamoke was doing."

Brian nodded.

"How many times have you been up," I said.

Bucko held up two fingers.

"Three would be a really unlucky number for you," I said.

Bucko shrugged and made his palms-up gesture again. Brian and I stood up. Brian gave Bucko his card.

"You find out anything to help your case," Brian said, "Give me a ringy dingy."

"Thank you for the coffee," I said.

When we were in Brian's car again, I said, "Mike didn't tell you Bucko sent him."

"I lied," Brian said.

"It's a lie might get Mike in trouble with Bucko," I said.

"What a shame," Brian said. "You believe Bucko?"

"He swore on his mother, didn't he?"

"Oh, yeah, I forgot."

He looked at his watch.

"That donut was enough," he said, "or can you eat some lunch?"

"I could eat some lunch," I said.

"Good."

CHAPTER 27

Spike was dressed for work when I got home. Millicent was on the couch in Spike's living room watching a talk show on television. Rosie rushed out of the living room when I opened the front door and chased her tail for a time before I picked her up and we exchanged kisses.

"I made her linguine with white clam sauce for lunch," Spike said. "She hated it."

"She's just not an educated eater," I said. "What did she have instead?"

"Crackers and peanut butter."

Spike's disgust was palpable.

"She'll learn," I said.

Spike took the big Army .45 from his hip pocket and handed it to me, butt first.

"Put that in my desk drawer," he said.

I took the gun and Spike went out the front door and closed it behind him. I put the gun away and went into the living room. On television two fat women wearing a lot of makeup were screaming at each other. Between them sat a skinny guy with a sparse beard and long hair. He looked pleased. I shut it off.

"I was listening," Millicent said.

"What are they fighting about," I said.

"He's married to one of them and cheating on her with the other one."

"He got two women to sleep with him?" I said.

"I guess so."

"You should never sleep with someone who can't grow a beard," I said.

"Why not?"

"Just sort of an anti-PC joke," I said.

"What's PC?"

"Politically correct," I said.

"What's that mean?"

I sat down and looked at her. Rosie jumped up and squeezed in beside me on the chair.

"I guess you could say it's a set of humorless rules about speech and behavior articulated publicly and privately meaningless."

"Sure," Millicent said. "You ever have sex with somebody that had a bad beard?"

I laughed.

"Not that I can recall."

"You have sex a lot?" Millicent said.

She was looking blankly at the inanimate television screen.

"Define 'a lot,' " I said.

"You know, do you screw a lot of guys?"

"If I like a man I am happy to sleep with him," I said. "But I don't meet that many men that I like."

"You have to like them?"

"Yep."

"Why have sex at all?"

I thought about that for a minute. It wasn't a question anyone had asked me in a while.

"Well, it feels nice," I said.

Millicent wrinkled her nose.

"And it is a kind of intimacy that is otherwise not possible."

"I never liked it," Millicent said.

"Well, the stuff when you were hooking doesn't count."

"Why not?"

"I assume there were no emotions involved. Nobody liked anybody. Just fucking. Just a commercial transaction. How about before that?"

"Couple of times with kids at school."

"Any special kid?"

"No, once with Chuck Sanders and Tommy Lee, and once with a guy named Roy."

"Chuck and Tommy at the same time?"

"Yeah, first one, then the other, in Tommy's car."

"Did you like them both?"

She shrugged.

"How about Roy, did you like him?"

"He was nice. Tommy and Chuck kind of hurt. Roy didn't so much."

"I think you need to suspend judgment on sex," I said. "Your experience is with fucking, not with lovemaking."

"What's the difference?"

"It's the difference between pleasure and pain," I said.

Millicent shrugged again. We were quiet. Rosie had rolled over on her back so I could rub her stomach.

"What do you like to do besides watch television?" I said.

"Nothing."

I could have given that answer for her.

"What do you think you know the most about?"

"I know a lot about getting by on the street," she said.

"Yes," I said. "You do. Anything else?"

She thought about it, but not for long. When she had stopped thinking, she shrugged.

"Street-smart is good," I said. "I find use for it myself. But if there were more than being street-smart, life would be more fun."

"Fun?"

"Yes. A foreign concept, I know. But one of the things that it is good to do in life is have fun."

"Like what?"

"Like being with people you love."

"Oh sure, like you?"

"I'm not," I said. "But I don't doubt its charm. It's also fun to love a dog, and look at art, and listen to music, and follow baseball, and go to the movies, and eat well, and read some books, and work out... stuff like that."

"That doesn't sound like fun to me."

"What's fun to you?" I said.

Millicent didn't say anything.

"You like Rosie?" I said.

"She's okay."

"God, don't let her hear you say that she's okay," I said. "She thinks she's the queen of cute."

Millicent smiled slightly. I was on a hot streak. We sat some more. The blank gray screen of Spike's television sat silently before us. Waiting.

"Let's make supper together," I said.

"I don't know how," Millicent said.

"Me either," I said. "We can get through it together."

Julie and I were having tea at a little place called LouLou's in Harvard Square near where Julie had her office.

"How awful for that girl," Julie said. "Can't you just turn it over to the police?"

"I'm working with a police detective on the men who came to my place. Brian says he can leave Millicent out of it for now. But I haven't told him about Millicent's mother."

Outside of LouLou's the pedestrians and motorists were having their ongoing stare down where Brattle Street wound down from the Square.

"Because?" Julie said.

"Because I have to know more about what's going on, before I put her in the position of testifying against her own mother."

"Brian's the police detective?"

"Un huh."

"Brian?"

"Yes."

"He cute?" Julie said.

"Quite."

"And?"

"And we had lunch the other day and I enjoyed it," I said.

"And?"

"And we'll see."

"Can Richie help you with this?" Julie said.

"With Brian?"

"No, not with Brian. Can he help you find out who sent those men to your loft."

"I'm already asking him to baby-sit," I said. "Divorce means going it on your own, I think."

"Being a professional means using the resources you have," Julie said.

"And Richie's a resource?"

"A good one. You know that."

"Yes. I do know that."

We were sharing a pot of Japanese sour cherry-flavored green tea. I poured some through the strainer for Julie and some for me.

"Is the girl a basket case?" Julie said.

"She doesn't have enough affect to be a basket case."

"She's withdrawn?"

"I don't know the therapy term for it. She doesn't know anything. No one seems to have taken any time to tell her anything. She has no interests. Love, sex, affection puzzle her. She doesn't like dogs."

"You can forgive her that?" Julie said.

"The dogs?" I said. "I'm trying to get past that."

"What does she do all day?"

"Watch television."

"Anything that's on?" Julie said.

"Anything."

"She's shut down," Julie said. "She can't handle the world she faces, so she effectively withdraws from it. Does she do drugs?"

"She had some pot with her when I grabbed her," I said. "But she smoked that. Since she's been with me she hasn't bought any."

"If she was using heavier stuff there'd be signs that she missed it," Julie said.

"That would be my guess, too."

My tea was gone.

"I'll have to get going soon," I said. "Spike's got to go to work."

Julie nodded.

"I wish I could help, but," she shrugged. "I can't have her with me. The kids, Michael? You know what Michael's like. He doesn't like anybody but me."

"I know. I wouldn't ask you."

"I guess I'm lucky he likes me so much," Julie said. "But it's not the easiest thing in the world to be someone's entire social life."

"I know."

"Sometimes we're having dinner, out, you know, nice place, and he's looking at me and I know he's wanting me to say something like Scarlett O'Hara or somebody. Something outrageously romantic."

"And you can't."

"And I can't," Julie said. "And I want to smack him for wanting me to."

"I know," I said. "Julie, I have to go. I've got to get back so Spike can leave."

"Like having a kid," Julie said.

"Without the pleasures of conception," I said.

"Or the pains of delivery," Julie said.

"On the other hand, you didn't have to shoot anybody," I said.

"Look at us arguing who's worse off," Julie said. "I'll admit I wouldn't trade places with you."

"Wait'll my sex life picks up," I said.

"Then I'll be jealous," Julie said.

We stood. I left some money on the table and we went out onto Brattle Street.

"Sunny," Julie said, as we walked up toward the T station in the square, "this is too hard to be proud about. Call Richie. See if he can help. You owe it to Millicent. You owe it to yourself. You owe it to Rosie."

"Rosie," I said.

Julie nodded.

"I hadn't thought about Rosie."

Julie nodded some more.

"I guess I'll have to call."

"Yes," Julie said, "you will."

CHAPTER 29

I was sitting with Bucko Meehan again, but this time Richie was with me. We were in a place off Rutherford Avenue which claimed that its steak tips were world-famous. Bucko was eating some. Richie and I were having coffee.

"Are they really world-famous?" I said.

Bucko drank some beer.

"They're great," he said. "You oughta try some."

"Not today."

"How's the family?" Bucko said to Richie.

"Fine," Richie said.

"Your father?"

Richie nodded.

"Your uncle?"

"Actually I got, as you know, five uncles," Richie said. "All of them are fine."

"Good," Bucko said, "good to hear that."

"My uncle Ernie was asking about you the other day," Richie said.

"He was? What?"

"Asking what I thought of you."

"Why's he want to know?"

Richie shrugged.

"You know Ernie," Richie said. "Doesn't talk a lot about things. Just asked my opinion of you."

"What'd you say?"

"Said I didn't have much opinion. Mostly just heard that you had talked to Sunny and hadn't been helpful."

"Sunny? Her?" Bucko nodded at me.

"Yeah."

"I didn't know she was a friend of yours, Richie."

"Now you do," Richie said.

I never knew how Richie got so much menace into things he said. He was very still, as he nearly always was. His voice was quiet. His face was calm.

"She was with a cop, Rich."

"Un huh."

"I was willing to help," Bucko said. "I just didn't have any answers."

"Un huh."

Bucko looked at me. I smiled adorably. Like Meg Ryan.

"I was wondering if you had any idea how Terry Nee ended up at my door with a gun?" I said.

"Like I told you..."

"Bucko," Richie said.

"Honest to God, Richie, I don't have a fucking clue."

"Bucko," Richie said.

"I don't."

"Think of it as me asking you, Buck."

"I unnerstan' that, Richie, but I don't."

"Think of what I'm going to have to tell my Uncle Ernie when he asks about you?"

"If I knew why Ernie was asking..." Bucko said.

Richie was quiet. I did my Meg Ryan smile again. Bucko had stopped eating his steak tips. A waitress came by and freshened our coffee cups. I added Equal and milk to mine. Richie added cream and sugar to his.

"Think about it this way," Richie said. "I'm asking you who sent Terry Nee to try and kill my wife."

"Your wife?"

"Ex," I said.

"Terry kicked my dog, too," Richie said. "And naturally I want to know how that came about. And I know Terry was with you."

"I didn't send him, Richie, I swear to Christ."

"I'm sure you didn't, Bucks, but you might have lent him to somebody and I'm going to find out who."

"She's ex anyway, ain't she?" Bucko said. "Didn't she just say that?"

Richie leaned across the table and put his hand on Bucko's forearm.

"She's family," Richie said. "As much as my father and my uncles and my brothers and me."

Richie didn't seem to be squeezing, but Bucko didn't seem able to get his arm away.

"You lent Terry Nee to somebody, didn't you?" Richie said softly.

Bucko was silent. I knew what was going on. He was trying to decide who he wanted mad at him. Richie's family, or the man who'd sent Terry Nee. He looked around the restaurant.

"Your word, you don't tell him where you got it?" Bucko said.

The devil who has hold of your forearm is better than the devil who's not around.

"My word," Richie said.

"Me too," I said.

"Cathal Kragan," Bucko said.

I looked at Richie. Richie shrugged.

"Who's Cathal Kragan," I said.

"Guy," Bucko said.

I opened my mouth. Richie shook his head

so briefly that I was sure only I had seen him. We waited.

"He represents some people," Bucko said. "I don't know who they are. But I see him around and I owe him a favor and he says he needs a little scuffle work done, nothing heavy, couple broads. And I say I can put him in touch with Terry and he says fine and so I do."

Bucko sat back as if he'd just said three Hail Marys and made a good Act of Contrition.

"Where do we find Cathal?" Richie said.

"He's around," Bucko said. "You know?"

"Can you get in touch with him?" I said.

Bucko shook his head.

"You know who he works for?" I said.

Bucko shook his head.

"But you're scared of them?"

"Don't know nothing about them," Bucko said. "I'm scared of Cathal."

"What's he look like?" I said.

"Thick," Bucko said. "Like me, a little shorter, gray hair. Got hands like a stonemason. Funny voice."

"Funny how?"

"I don't know exactly. It's real deep."

Richie took his hand off Bucko's forearm.

"My Uncle Ernie will be glad to hear you were helpful," Richie said.

"Give him my best," Bucko said. "Your father, too."

"Sure," Richie said.

We stood. Richie dropped a hundred-dollar bill on the table.

"No, no, Richie," Bucko said. "I got it."

Richie took my arm and we walked away without answering.

"You ever hear of Cathal Kragan?" I said in the car.

"Nope."

We were crossing the Charlestown Bridge.

"What kind of name is Cathal?" I said.

"Irish," Richie said. "There was a guy during the troubles named Cathal Brugha."

"How do you know that?" I said.

"I read a book."

"Well," I said. "Good for you."

And we laughed together as we passed the Fleet Center and Richie turned right onto Causeway Street.

CHAPTER 30

Whenever I skipped rope I had to block Rosie out of the room because otherwise she would attempt to participate. I was skipping rope, wearing tights and a tank top in Spike's living room while Millicent watched television and Rosie sat in the hallway, humped up like a skunk in the fog, looking at me balefully.

"How come you're doing that?" Millicent said.

"I can't get to the gym," I said.

I kept skipping as I talked, trying not to sound winded.

"Because of me?"

"Yes."

"So why'nt you just forget it?"

"Several reasons," I said. "I try to stay in shape, for, ah, professional reasons. I like to eat and drink, but I am vain about my appearance and I don't want to put on weight... also I'm compulsive about it."

"My mother's always exercising," Millicent said.

"Would you like to try it?"

She shook her head.

"Didn't you ever skip rope when you were little?" I said.

She shrugged. I stopped skipping and dropped down on Spike's rug and did some push-ups.

"Have you ever done push-ups?" I said.

"Girls don't do push-ups," she said with scorn of an intensity only adolescent girls can achieve.

"Women do," I said.

"Well, I guess I'm not a woman."

"Maybe you are," I said. "Try one."

She shook her head. I kept doing them.

"Try one," I said.

"I can't do them. They tried to make us in gym once."

"They didn't do it right," I said. "Get down here. I'll show you."

Millicent dragged herself off the couch and flopped down on the floor on her stomach.

"Okay," I said. "Start with a half push-up. Put your hands out like this, and push up, but leave your knees on the floor."

She did what I said and pushed her torso up and let it down.

"Okay?" she said.

"See, you can do it," I said. "Try five."

She looked disgusted, but she did five.

"Excellent," I said.

Millicent got up and went back and flopped on the couch. I finished my push-ups and got up and went to the door and moved the footstool, and Rosie trotted into the room and wagged at us. I picked her up and gave her a kiss and let her lap my neck.

"How come she doesn't just jump over the footstool?" Millicent said. "Can't she jump?"

"She can," I said. "But she doesn't know it. She thinks she can't, so she doesn't try."

Millicent looked at me and didn't say anything. I smiled at her innocently.

"You think I'm like that?" Millicent said.

"Sorry," I said. "But you handed it to me."

"But you do think I'm like that."

"You were like that about the push-ups," I said.

"I didn't do a real push-up," Millicent said.

"You did six real half push-ups," I said. "We work on it regularly and in a while you'll do some real full push-ups."

"So what? I hate doing push-ups."

"If you can do them, then you can decide if you want to do them. If you can't do them, the decision isn't yours."

Millicent frowned, as if I'd said something mathematical that she suspected was correct but she didn't understand the terms.

"Who cares about push-ups?" she said.

"It's more sort of an attitude," I said. "The more things you can do, the more choices you have. The more choices you have, the less life kicks you around."

"So I do push-ups, my life will be better?"

"It's better to be strong than weak," I said. "And it's better to be quick than slow. But you're not stupid; you know I mean something a little larger."

She shrugged again and picked up the clicker and changed channels on the television set.

"You don't think I'm stupid?" Millicent said.

"No. I think you are probably pretty smart. It's just that no one has taught you much."

"Like what?"

"Like how to be a person," I said.

"You think you know?"

"Um hm."

"So what makes you so smart?"

"It's not smart, it's learning."

"I hate school," Millicent said.

"Me, too," I said. "Mostly I've learned stuff from my father and from Richie and from my friend Julie and Spike and Rosie and from being alive and paying attention for thirty-five years. I have plenty more to learn. I need to get my love life straightened out, for instance. But I have more information than you do. I have enough to take care of myself."

"You learned stuff from Rosie?"

"Yes. How to pay attention, how to take care of someone without owning them..."

"But you do own her."

"I bought her," I said. "But I don't own her. I feed her, I give her water. I take her to the vet. I let her out and in. I take her for walks. The truth of it is she'd die if I didn't take care of her. And because she's completely dependent on me, I am determined that within the confines of what I just said, and allowing for her safety and mine, she can live as she wishes and do as she pleases."

"But you just shut her out of the room."

"Life's imperfect," I said. "I wish it weren't."

"Why don't you train her not to bite the jump rope."

"I think that imposes on her more than shutting her out," I said.

"You think stuff like this all the time?"

"Sometimes I think about clothes and makeup and guys," I said. "Want to talk about them?"

"I don't know much about that either," Millicent said.

"Yet."

She shrugged. I hated shrugging.

CHAPTER 31

Cathal Kragan had no record. Brian had never heard of him. Neither had anybody in the organized crime unit. The name meant nothing to Millicent. Using Spike's computer I checked out Brock Patton on the Internet.

"Be careful," Spike said. "You download the wrong thing and you'll be in the middle of my sex life."

"At least you have one," I said.

"We feeling a little deprived, are we?"

"Maybe just a little."

"Too bad I'm not in your program," Spike said. "Think of the symphony we could make."

"It's always something," I said. "What's your password?"

He told me and I punched it in and went online. After much more diddling around than the computer ads would allow you to imagine, I located Brock Patton. He was in among all the listings on the planet that contained the words Brock or Patton. I got a zillion articles on General Patton, and several on a football player named Brock Marion, and quite a few on an actor named Brock Peters, and a politician named Brock, and two on a football player named Peter Brock, and another one named Stan Brock, who appeared to be Peter's brother, and, buried among them, five or six on the guy I was actually trying to find.

Here was the CEO of MassBay Trust which was the ninth-biggest bank in the country. Before that he'd been the president of the biggest bank in Rhode Island. He had been a very active Republican fund-raiser in both Rhode Island and Massachusetts. He had served the last Republican administration as

Commerce Secretary, and it was said that he would be the Republican candidate for governor in two years. He was also a world-class trap shooter, and a Harvard graduate. There was one article about Betty Patton as a ferocious fund-raiser for several deserving charities. There were no pictures of Betty Patton in the buff. There was no mention of anyone named Cathal Kragan. None of the articles mentioned a disaffected daughter.

I sat back in the swivel chair in Spike's den and stared at the blue green screen of Spike's seventeen-inch Sony monitor. I was alone. Spike and Millicent had taken Rosie for a walk. I had insisted that Millicent wear a hat and sunglasses. Spike said there was not much chance someone would even be cruising the South End looking for her, and if they were, they would have an even smaller chance of recognizing her. I said they might recognize Rosie and put it together. Spike said maybe I overrated Rosie's visibility. Rosie meanwhile was jumping up in the air and turning around before she landed and biting her leash. Rosie loved to walk. She would have gone for a walk with Dracula. Millicent seemed, if not eager, at least not resistant. Anything she wasn't resistant to was to be encouraged. Spike reminded me that Millicent would be with him and that he was both fearless and deadly. So I said okay, and Spike stuck the big Army .45 in his belt under his jacket and off they went. I had to admit I liked being alone. Maybe my judgment had swayed a little.

I had known that Brock Patton was a banker, but the fact that he might make a run for governor gave new urgency to the knowledge that his wife posed for dirty pictures, and his daughter had been, if briefly, a hooker. I could see why he would want to keep a lid on things. I could see why his wife would. But why did Cathal Kragan care? What I knew was, there was a scheme under way. Maybe about being governor, maybe about something else. But there were people willing to kill somebody in the interests of that scheme, and Betty Patton was in on it.

I could ask her, but she wouldn't tell me and then they'd know I knew, which would make everything harder, including not getting killed. I called my answering machine on my cell phone. Even if someone were able to trace the call they wouldn't know where I was. There was a call from Brian. There was also a call from an attorney who said he represented Brock Patton. I broke the connection and dialed Brian's number.

"Somebody aced Bucko Meehan," he said when I got him. "This morning, early."

"Suspects?"

"None."

"How?"

"In his bed. Shot in the middle of the forehead. .357 Mag. Bullet came out the back and through the mattress and buried in the floor boards under the bed."

"Who found him?"

"Cleaning woman, had her own key. Let herself in about 9:30 this morning and there he was."

"How nice for her," I said.

"You know anything I don't know?" Brian said.

"No. Somebody must have seen him talking to us," I said.

"My guess," Brian said. "Unless it was somebody your ex sent over."

"No. Richie's not a criminal," I said.

"He comes from a criminal family," Brian said.

"I know. But it doesn't mean he's one."

"The way you tell it, he used that criminal family to squeeze Bucko for you."

"Yes. But he wouldn't have anyone killed. Besides, what good would that do any of us. He was our only link to Cathal Kragan."

"And now he's not," Brian said.

"So maybe Richie's an unlikely suspect."

"Yeah, maybe he is."

"You sound like you wish he were a suspect," I said.

"Just trying to get something to grab hold of," Brian said. "I'm not picking on Richie."

"Good," I said.

"I thought you were divorced," Brian said.

"I am. But that doesn't make me silly."

"For sure," Brian said. "You want to have dinner?"

"Let me get my book," I said.

I got it.

"I'm open every night until 2003," I said. "What's good for you?"

CHAPTER 32

I thought there might be more to Brock Patton than one saw in the presence of his wife, so I went down to the MassBay building on State Street during business hours and took the elevator to his offices on the top floor. His secretary had on a little black Donna Karan suit and some pearls. She was very attractive, and felt good about it. She took my card with just enough contempt to remind me who was who, and read my name into the phone. She listened for a moment, allowed her surprise to show in a tasteful fashion and stood to usher me in.

Patton greeted me at the door.

"Sunny Randall," he said. "A pleasure."

He gestured me in and spoke to his secretary.

"I don't want to be disturbed," he said and closed the door.

The office was about the size of a major cathedral in a poor country. There was a wet bar on the right-hand wall. Beyond it a door opened into what appeared to be a full bath. A sofa big enough to sleep two was against the left-hand wall, and opposite the wet bar was a desk on which pygmies could easily play soccer. The rug was dark green. The walls were burgundy. The sofa and several armchairs were in some sort of butterscotch leather.

The wall opposite the door was glass and through it I could see Boston Harbor and the Atlantic beyond and the shoreline as far south as Patagonia. On the walls were pictures of Brock with bird dogs and dead pheasants, Brock with important people, Brock firing shotguns. Where there were no pictures there were plaques, which honored Brock's skeet-shooting skills. On some shelves there were shooting trophies. There were no pictures of Betty Patton, and none of Millicent.

"I must say I'm surprised to see you, Sunny," Brock said.

"We have a common interest," I said.

"You haven't been acting as if we did," he said.

He had his coat off, hanging somewhere in a closet, but otherwise he was in full uniform: striped shirt with a tab collar, pink silk tie, pink-flowered suspenders, blue pinstripe suit pants, black wing tips.

"I suppose it's argumentative, but neither have you," I said.

"Goddamn," he said. "You're a scrappy little bitch."

"Thanks for thinking so, you have any idea why armed men would be trying to find your daughter?"

"Armed men?" he raised his eyebrows.

"I killed one of them," I said.

Brock stared at me for a while.

"Killed, how?" he finally said.

"With a ten-gauge shotgun," I said.

He stared at me some more.

"You care to tell me about it?"

"No. I want you to tell me who these men might be."

"How... the hell... would I know that?"

"His name was Terry Nee. Worked for a man named Bucko Meehan."

"Never heard of either of them."

"Someone killed Bucko yesterday."

"Jesus, Sunny, what the hell have you got me into?"

"I think it's the other way around. Ever hear of a man named Cathal Kragan?"

"Who?"

"Cathal Kragan. It's an Irish name."

"No, Sunny, I've never heard of him. Have you discussed all this with the police?"

"How is your marriage?" I said.

"My marriage?"

I nodded.

"Why are you interested?"

"Mr. Patton..."

"Brock," he said.

"Brock. I don't know what's going on here and I'm trying to find out. So I ask questions... like, are you and your wife happily married?"

He let his chair lean back, behind his vast desk, and folded his hands across his flat stomach. His hands were strong-looking, and tanned, the hands of an outdoorsman, but manicured. He was freshly shaved. I could smell his cologne. His color was good. His clothes fit him beautifully. His teeth were even and very white when he smiled at me.

"Let me say, Sunny, that I'm not so married that I wouldn't respond to you."

"Who could be that married?" I said. "You can't think of any reason Millicent took off?"

"Don't know, Sunny, and, you might as well know the truth, don't much goddamned care."

"I sort of guessed that," I said.

"Since she was born she's never been right. Schools and shrinks and trouble and more shrinks and different schools and more trouble and money, Christ, has she cost us money."

"So why'd you hire me to find her?"

"Well, hell, you can't just abandon her. I mean, how the hell does that look, your daughter runs off and you don't even look for her."

"How's it look to whom?" I said.

"To anybody."

"To the voters?"

"Sure, to the voters; it's no secret I want to be governor. I can't have my daughter out hooking on the damned streets while I'm running for public office, for crissake."

"So now you know she's not hooking, but you don't know where she is. Is that driving you crazy?"

"I got half a mind to pull your pants off and fuck you right here on the couch," he said.

"That is about half a mind," I said.

We stared at each other for a time.

"What do you want?" he said.

"Anything that will help me figure out how to help your daughter."

"I don't know anything. Why don't you just hop right onto that couch and we'll see how much woman you are."

"I love it when you're poetic," I said. "Am I still working for you?"

He grinned. It was a very ugly grin for a man so handsome. It was a grin without humor, or friendliness. It was only a gesture he made with his mouth as he stared at a fresh piece of meat.

"Depends," he said, "On how quick you hop on the couch."

"Does your wife cheat on you?" I said.

Again the fresh-meat grin. His blue eyes seemed smaller, and the pupils seemed shrunken.

"Why would she?" he said.

"Women are so flighty," I said.

He stood up.

"Maybe you like it rough," he said. "Maybe I'll just toss you onto that couch."

I stood up, too.

"Remember the clay pigeon," I said.

"You saying you'd shoot me?"

"Right in your little peenie," I said.

He took a step around his desk. I pulled the gun from under my coat. He stopped. We looked at each other. Then he snorted and sat back down.

"You missed your chance, bitch."

"And I hope to miss it again," I said, and went to the office door and opened it and walked out and left it open behind me.

CHAPTER 33

I got the address of her shrink from Millicent, and made an appointment.

Her office was on the second floor of a small commercial building in Wellesley next door to a physical therapy center. Sound in mind and body, one-stop shopping. The sign on her door said Marguerite Sandborn, Family Counseling. I went in and sat in her empty waiting room for maybe ten minutes before her inner office door opened, and a woman I assumed to be Marguerite held it open while a much younger woman came from the inner office and walked past me and out with her eyes fixed firmly on the floor ahead of her. When the young woman was gone, Marguerite invited me in, and told me to call her Marguerite.

"I must warn you, Ms. Randall, that transactions between myself and a client are strictly confidential."

"Strictly," I said.

"Within that guideline, I am happy to help."

"Excellent," I said. "Millicent Patton was your patient."

"I prefer the term client," Marguerite said.

She had long, graying hair. She wore a shapeless dress with big flowers on it, and no makeup. The only jewelry was a narrow gold wedding band on her left hand. She looked exactly the way a mental health professional ought to look, one who had rejected the artifice of ordinary women to embrace the deeper beauty. I was very glad I hadn't done the same thing.

"She was your client?" I said.

"She is still my client," Marguerite said. "She just isn't coming to see me at the moment."

"Right. Did you know that she had run away from home?"

Marguerite paused for a moment. Then she said, "I'm not surprised."

I raised my eyebrows and looked interested, and waited.

"She was…" Marguerite paused thoughtfully. "She had failed to live up to her parents' expectations. Her parents were disappointed. Millicent resented their expectations and their disappointment and was very angry."

"And what was your job?" I said.

Marguerite smiled at me the way professionals do when an amateur asks them a question. "To help her see that her parents expectations were not unreasonable, to see that she was perfectly capable of achieving them, and to help her deal with her anger."

"She have any expectations for herself?" I said.

Marguerite shook her head very slightly, as if a fly had landed on her ear. She didn't answer. Apparently the head twitch dismissed the question.

"She a good patient?" I said.

Marguerite smiled sadly, "She was resistant."

"To the idea that her parents' expectations weren't unreasonable?"

"If you wish," Marguerite said. "It is a bit more complex than that."

"Of course," I said. "How did you do with her anger?"

"We were making some progress. We took a few moments every session to help her drain some of it off."

"How?" I said, "if it's not privileged."

"No, no. It's not privileged," Marguerite said. "I use it with many clients."

She nodded toward the corner of the room where a small body bag stood on a pedestal with a pair of boxing gloves hanging from a hook next to it.

"She hit the body bag?" I said.

"Yes. She was free to imagine it was anyone she wished."

"She say anything when she was punching the bag?" I said.

"I'm sorry, that would be privileged."

"But she did say things?"

"Not very much." Marguerite said. "It was a rather silent fury."

"But she did give the bag a good punching out?"

"Yes."

"Like she liked it?"

"Yes."

"Do we call that displacement?" I said.

Again the indulgent smile. How sweet the way I tried to understand the magic she performed.

"How'd she get here?" I said.

"I believe one of the servants drove her. A maid."

"Can you tell me if she was close to anyone?"

"We didn't spend much time on such matters," Marguerite said. "I think she might have liked the maid who drove her, maybe a little."

"You know her name?"

"I don't recall."

"You have any notes, whatever, that might tell us?"

"I never take notes," Marguerite said. "I try to give myself fully to the client. Empathy is crucial."

I was pretty sure that a certain amount of distance was also useful, but I didn't think it would be productive to argue that point. As we talked I glanced at the framed document on the wall. The best I could make out from the Latinate mumbo jumbo in which they were written was she had a B.A. from North Dakota State, and an M.Ed. from Lesley College.

"Do you happen to know if there is more than one maid?"

"I believe there is a butler and a maid."

"And the butler is a guy?"

"That is my impression."

"Is there anything else you can tell me that will help me to understand her?"

"Perhaps you should be more concerned with finding her," Marguerite said.

"I have found her."

"Then why on earth... ?"

"I'm trying to figure out what to do with her."

"You haven't returned her to her parents."

"She doesn't want to go."

"And you feel that her wishes are sufficiently mature."

"Yeah."

"And you feel that it is your responsibility to honor them?"

"Yes."

"I hope you do not exceed your expertise," Marguerite said.

I thought about taking a turn on the body bag. But I had too much detecting to do. Displacement would have to wait.

"Me, too," I said.

CHAPTER 34

Most of the time when I tail somebody, it's in the city, and on foot, and it's not especially hard to do if they don't know you by sight. But out in the wilds of South Natick, near the Dover line, where no one is on foot, and the Pattons would recognize me on sight, it was a somewhat larger proposition. I got out my collection of street maps and drove around the area until I had a pretty good idea of what roads led where and what was parallel to what. Then I parked off the road at the end of the dead-end street that ran past the Patton's long driveway and waited. It took about two hours before a Natick Cruiser pulled up behind me and a young cop got out and walked up beside the car, staying a little behind me on the driver's side. By the time he got there I had my papers out and the window down.

He said, "May I see your license and registration, please."

I handed them out, along with my detective license. The cop was quite cute, with little crinkles at the corners of his eyes. He was very young. Was he too young for me? Hideous thought.

"I'm working an undercover thing with the Boston Police," I said. "You can call Sergeant Brian Kelly, District 6 detectives, and ask him."

"What might that undercover thing be?" he said.

"We're suspicious of one of your residents, but it may not pan out, and we don't want to hurt anyone's reputation until we know."

"Wait here, please."

He walked back to the cruiser and was on the radio for a long time. I didn't mind waiting. I was waiting anyway. Eventually the young cop strolled back from his cruiser to my car and handed my papers back to me.

"Took awhile to get Kelly," he said. "But we did and he vouches for you. Talked to my chief, too. He says you can stay here long as we don't get any complaints. But you annoy somebody or we get too many calls about you hanging around the neighborhood, we're going to have to respond."

"Sure," I said.

"Boston cops hiring a lot of private eyes these days?"

"Just happens that our interests coincide on this case."

"Well, you need some help, give us a call," he said.

He turned and strolled back to his cruiser, the way cops do, sort of sauntering as if they had all the time in the world. I watched him as he went. He backed up carefully, and pulled out around me and waved and drove away. Young... but not impossible.

I sat some more. It was full-out autumn now. A lot of the trees were bare. The leaves that had fallen littered the road and packed drably along the sides of the road. The leaves that hadn't fallen were bright gold with some splashes here and there of red. After another hour and a half, a small red Ford Escort came down the street that ran past the Pattons' house and turned right, onto my street. The driver was a good-looking black woman. I'd seen her twice now when I called on her employers, and, being a trained observer, I recognized her as the Patton's maid. When she drove past, I slid out behind her and trailed along after her as she turned right in South Natick Center and drove along Route 16 through Wellesley and parked in the lot beside Bread & Circus.

She went in. I went in behind her. Turned left where she had turned right, went down an aisle and came up to her as if by accident.

"Hello," I said. "Small world."

She looked at me uncertainly.

"Sunny Randall," I said. "I'm doing some work for the Pattons."

"Oh, yes, ma'am, how nice to see you."

"It's nice to see you. Do you have a minute so I could buy you a cup of coffee?"

"Well, I really need to shop, Ms. Randall, and get back for supper."

"It won't take long. I need to talk to you a little about Millicent."

"My Millicent?"

"Millicent Patton," I said.

She was very good-looking, with big dark eyes and smooth skin. She was wearing a nice perfume. In jeans and a white tee shirt she might have been a Wellesley College senior, though if you looked closely you could see a little more age than that at the corners of her eyes and mouth. She looked regretfully at her carriage, which, so far, had accumulated a head of broccoli.

"There's a place next door," she said finally.

"Good, thank you."

When we were seated and had our coffee, I said, "I don't know your name."

"My real name is Elinor, but everyone calls me Billie."

"Last name?"

"Otis."

"My real name's Sonya," I said.

176

"Yes, ma'am."

"Please call me Sunny. Could you tell me a little about Millicent."

Her eyes were steady as she looked at me.

"We don't talk about our employers," Billie said.

"You being who?"

"My husband and I."

"Your husband is the butler?"

"Yes."

"His name?"

"John."

"John Otis?"

"Yes."

I drank some coffee.

"I understand," I said, "and I admire, your reticence. But I need help. She's in bigger trouble than any fifteen-year-old kid ought to be, and I can only help her by understanding her and her family."

"You know where she is?" Billie said.

"Yes."

"She all right?"

"She's not hurt, and for the moment she's safe," I said. "I understand that you used to drive her to counseling twice a week."

"Yes, ma'am."

"Billie, we're both employees. No need to ma'am me. My name is Sunny."

Billie nodded.

"You drove her to therapy."

"Yes."

"Her parents ever drive her?"

"No."

"Too busy?"

"I guess."

"You and she ever talk about things when you were driving her back and forth?"

"Some."

"What did you talk about?"

Billie looked straight at me for a moment, her big dark eyes full of the knowledge of things I'd never encountered. "This is a good job, Miss Randall. Good money. John and I get to work together. We get most weekends off together. Lot of couples work domestic, they never get time off together."

"You like Millicent?" I said.

"I feel bad for her," Billie said.

"Because?"

"Because she's so alone. Got nobody to talk to."

"Except you?"

Billie didn't answer.

"Billie, she needs us to help her."

"You first," Billie said. "What kind of trouble is she in?"

"There are men trying to find her. Men with guns. I had to kill one."

Billie's face never changed.

"There's something going on involving her mother," I said, "maybe her father, and I think it's why these men are after her. I think it's why she ran away."

"I don't know anything about that," Billie said.

"You know a man named Cathal Kragan?"

She picked her coffee cup up in both hands

and drank some and put the cup back down and sat back in the wooden booth.

"Yes."

"How?"

"If I tell you things, will it help Millicent?"

"It might," I said. "I don't know."

"You don't lie, do you?" Billie said.

"Actually I do," I said. "But this didn't seem the time."

"He's been to the house." Billie said. "It's not a name you forget."

"Has he been alone?"

"Sometimes alone. Once with another man."

"What was the other man's name?"

"I don't remember; he only came once."

"What did he look like?"

"He was so out of place. French cuffs, spread collar, silk tie, alligator shoes—the shoes had lifts in them, you could tell. His nails were manicured."

"Old, young, middle-aged?"

"Middle-aged. And the other funny thing, he was the boss."

"How do you know?"

"The way he was. The way the other man was, the Kragan man."

"Did they come to see Mr. or Mrs.?" I said.

"Both. I brought them into the study, where I brought you, and Mr. and Mrs. Patton were both in there."

"Did they say anything?"

"No."

"When Kragan came to visit alone did he always call on them both?"

"Usually. Except once, he just wanted to see Mrs. Patton."

"Which was the day Millicent ran away."

"I guess so."

"Did they love their daughter?" I said.

"I don't... how can I say?"

"You're not testifying in court, Billie," I said. "What do you think? Do you think they loved her?"

She sat with her coffee cup in her hands and looked at me. I waited. The small movement in the coffee shop seemed far away. She began to shake her head, and as she shook it, her eyes dampened.

"No," she said.

"Did they ever?"

"Maybe her momma did once."

"Did they love each other?"

"Oh God, no."

"Did they ever?"

"I haven't been there forever."

"But not since you've been there?"

"No."

"Did they fool around?"

"You mean sexually, with other people?"

"Yes."

"Miss Randall, I can't..."

"Sure you can. You care enough about the kid to tear up over the fact that her parents don't love her. And, damn it, call me Sunny."

Again the long pause. My coffee, still half a cup, was cold. I waited.

"They both brought people home," she

said. "If one of them was away the other would bring in a guest."

"How about Millicent?"

"They didn't seem to care if she knew."

"Did they know?"

"About each other?"

"Um hmm."

"I don't know. They weren't very careful. They didn't seem to care if John or I knew."

"Know any of the people that they brought home?"

"No."

"Were they people who came often or did they go for variety?"

"Variety, I'm afraid."

"Both of them?"

"Yes."

"Kragan or the other man didn't happen to leave a business card?"

"No."

"You notice the kind of car they drove? Or the license number?"

"No. John might have noticed the car. I'm sure he wouldn't have noticed the license number."

"How about the various one-night stands?" I said. "How did they come?"

"I don't know. John might."

"Will you ask John these things?" I said. "And have him call me?"

"Why do you want to know?"

"Because I don't know. It's sort of like panning for gold. You get a bunch of dirt and then you sort through it, see if there's a nugget."

"If Mrs. Patton finds out I spoke with you, John and I will be fired."

"How about Mr. Patton?"

"I don't know. Mrs. Patton runs the house."

"Neither will ever hear it from me," I said.

Billie nodded. I put my hand out and patted her hands where they lay folded in front of her on the table.

"We're going to save this kid, Billie."

Billie stared at the cold coffee in the bottom of her cup and said nothing.

CHAPTER 35

Millicent and I were getting stir-crazy, so we went to the gym with Spike. I put my .38 along with his .45 in his gym bag. Spike kept the gym bag unzipped and nearby as we went through the workouts.

Millicent wore a pair of shorts that belonged to me, and one of her new tee shirts. She was very slim. Her small body looked very white, and somehow incomplete in the workout clothes. The club was nearly empty in the middle of the day. Millicent stared around her at the exercise equipment.

"Girls don't go to gyms," Millicent said. "Why not?"

"I mean, who wants to lift weights and shit?"

"Great way to meet guys, though," Spike said.

He was barefoot, in full karate whites, with his black belt tied around his waist to keep the jacket closed.

Millicent stared at him. She hadn't figured Spike out yet. She wasn't alone in that.

"Besides, I don't know how to do it," Millicent said.

"Nobody does until they've learned," I said. "We'll show you."

"You lift weights?"

"Not very heavy ones," I said.

Spike dropped down onto the chest press machine and began to do repetitions with 225 pounds.

"Come on," I said. "First we'll do some push-ups like I showed you."

She got down onto the floor awkwardly and did some half push-ups with me. No one paid any attention to us. When we got through Spike was still doing repetitions on the chest press machine.

"How many of those are you doing, Spike?"

He held the weight at arm's length for a moment.

"I'm up to twenty-eight," he said. "Some pro football player did forty-five, so I'm eventually going to do forty-six." He grinned and lowered the bar. "But not today."

"Can I try how heavy that is?" Millicent said.

Spike showed her how to get under the bar.

"Okay," he said, "Breathe in, then while you exhale, push up."

Millicent did as he told her with no result.

"I can't," she said. "How come you can?"

"Fag power," Spike said.

"I thought you weren't supposed to call gay people fags," Millicent said.

"Sticks and stones," Spike said.

Millicent relinquished her spot to him.

"You are gay, aren't you?"

"Gayer than laughter," Spike said.

He began to do another set of chest presses. Millicent watched him.

"You seem like kind of a tough guy," she said.

"Hard to figure, isn't it?" Spike said.

I began to do some curls with ten-pound weights.

"Well, I mean, I never think of gay guys as tough."

Spike let the bar down and sat up on the bench to let his breathing normalize.

"It's sort of hard to generalize about gay guys," Spike said. "Some fit the stereotype, some don't. I prefer to have sex with men, and other than that I just kind of plow along and do what I do and don't think too much about it."

Millicent looked at me.

"Are those weights heavy?"

"For me," I said. "You want to try?"

She didn't say anything but she took the dumbbells when I handed them to her.

"Palms out," I said. "Hold them straight down in front of your thighs. Now using your bicep curl them slowly up toward your shoulders."

She did it.

"Good, now let them down slowly and do it again. Don't heave. If you have to sway, it's too heavy. Concentrate on just the biceps."

She did another one.

"See how many you can do before you start to cheat."

"Cheat?"

"You know, arch your back, sway your shoulders. The body is very clever about shifting the load."

She did three more.

"Good," I said.

"Okay, I can do that, so what?"

"In a while if you keep doing it you'll get stronger, and your arms will firm up."

"I don't want to get big muscles."

"You won't. You don't have the right hormones."

"So what's the point?"

"Be stronger, look better, feel good."

Millicent shrugged. "Women don't have to be strong."

"Better than being weak," I said.

I went to the Gravitron and set it for my weight and did some dips and some pull-ups.

"Want to try this?"

"Okay."

I set the Gravitron higher so that she'd feel very light. She did the same things I had done. I didn't tell her that her setting was lighter. We did some triceps exercises and some flys and some leg work and then we sat side by side on a couple of exercise bikes and rode for twenty minutes. When we got through she was winded. We drank some water, and watched Spike do karate work on the heavy bag.

"You do this every day?"

"Many days," I said. "Sometimes I can't get the time, then I don't."

"You do it because you're a detective," Millicent said.

"I'd do it anyway. I like to be in shape as much as I can be."

"Why?"

"It's healthy. It makes me feel good. And..." I paused, trying to think about it.

"What?"

"And... I'm not just my body. But it's part of what I am. I want it to be a good body. I want my mind to be a good mind. I want my emotions to be good emotions. I'm all there is of me, if you see what I'm saying, I want to make the most of me."

"I don't think about stuff like that, Sunny. I don't even know anybody who thinks about stuff like that."

I grinned at her.

"It's because they haven't had you around asking them questions."

"Do we have to take a shower here?" Millicent said.

"No," I said. "We can take one at Spike's."

"I don't like getting undressed in front of people."

"A possible handicap in your former profession," I said.

"I didn't like it," she said. "I didn't think about it. I never think about stuff."

Spike moved around the heavy bag, striking it with those odd precise movements that karate people use. Then he moved to the light one and made it rattle.

"Good for hand speed," he said to us.

He finished with a flourish, making the bag syncopate.

"Well, it's time you started thinking about stuff," I said. "Want to try the bag?"

"The one Spike was just hitting? The big one?"

"Sure."

"Can I just hit it, any way I want?"

"Sure. Just like at Marguerite's office."

Millicent looked at me as if she wanted to ask what Marguerite had said. But she didn't. Spike took off the speed gloves he was using and handed them to her.

"They're sweaty," she said.

"Yeah, but you hit that thing without them and you'll skin your knuckles."

She shrugged and put on the gloves and began to flail at the bag. She lasted about twenty seconds. Spike looked at me.

"There's a way to hit the bag," I said.

"You said I could hit it any way I want."

"You can. But now you can't decide. You hit it that way because you have to. If you learn another way, then you can choose."

"Jesus, you never get off it, do you," Millicent said.

"Choice is good," Spike said.

I took the gloves from Millicent and began to hit the bag.

"Shorter punches," Spike said to Millicent. "See? Keep the arms in kind of close, so you get mostly body into it instead of all arm. Loop one, Sunny."

I looped a punch the way Millicent had.

"See, all arm," Spike said. "You swing wide like that and you get the weight of your arm. Maybe five pounds? Show her a good one, Sunny."

I dug a left hook into the bag, exaggerating the shoulder turn to make the point.

"But, you punch short," Spike said, "like that, and you get all of you, more than 100 pounds, behind the punch."

He gave her the gloves back. She began to flail at the bag. Spike shook his head and opened his mouth.

I said, "Let's get some water." Spike shrugged and went with me to the water cooler.

"All you can do is show her the right way," I said. "Once she knows, it's up to her."

Spike stared across the room at Millicent, flogging the bag badly.

"She's just being stubborn," he said.

"So are you," I said.

"Yeah, but I'm right," he said.

"She knows that," I said. "What the hell do you think she's being stubborn about?"

Spike grinned at me.

"Shooter, shrink, painter, and sex symbol." Spike said. "You're a broad for all seasons, Sunny."

"Dog handler, too," I said.

36

I left Spike and Millicent debating whether Spike should make lobster fricassee for lunch, or if they should go out for a sub sandwich. I took Rosie with me and drove over to my loft. My answering machine wasn't working and I wanted to check on that, and check my mail, and, in truth, I wanted Rosie and me to walk around in our own space for a little while.

Alone.

I parked in front, put Rosie on her leash, and got out of the car. Rosie was excited. It was her home, too. She squatted a couple of times to reestablish herself, and then she and I went in and up the stairs.

My door was jimmied and ajar.

I switched Rosie's leash to my left hand and took my gun out, and cocked it, and pushed the door open with my foot. Rosie sniffed in ahead of me, her tail wagging furiously. I stayed close to the wall and slid through behind her. The loft was chaos. There was no sound. I saw no one. Rosie strained on the leash, sniff, sniff, sniffing. I squatted with my gun still cocked, and my back to the wall just inside the door, and unsnapped her leash. She dashed into the loft and raced around sniffing everything. I knew her very well. If there had been anyone there she would have acted differently. I relaxed a little and stood. My front door lock was broken, but there was a slide bolt on the inside which still worked and I used it. With my gun still out, and the hammer still back, I checked behind the counter in the kitchen, and under the bed, and in the bathroom. Rosie was right. There was no one there. I let the hammer down gently and put the gun back in its holster and looked at the mess someone had made of my loft. It was more than someone looking for something. It was vandalism. Every drawer was emptied. My clothes were all over the floor. Olive oil and molasses and flour and maybe ketchup and who knew what else had been dumped on them. My answering machine was broken on the floor. My mail had been opened and discarded. All my files were dumped and strewn. Most of the paper had been torn up. The bed had been torn apart, and someone had slashed the mattress open. My makeup had been emptied into the sink. I walked to the studio section. My easel was broken, the painting of Chinatown slashed. The three other canvases I had were torn and slashed. The paint was squeezed from the tubes all over the floor.

In the kitchen my glassware had been broken on the floor. My spice shelf had been emptied. My refrigerator door was open and the half quart of milk I had left there was curdled. Rosie was very excited. She was dashing around happily lapping the oil and molasses that had been poured. I picked her up and held her in my lap and sat on the only chair still upright.

They had come in probably trying to find

a clue to where I was with Millicent, and as they had searched and not found a clue, they had gotten excited and vengeful and this was what they'd left me. It was so unfair. It was like junior high school vandalism, simply mean. The vandals got no benefit from destroying my home, and all my things that I had so carefully picked out. All the things I had arranged and rearranged over whole evenings of puttering and reputtering, just me and Rosie, like a kid playing house, after Richie and I had separated. I was alone for the first time in my life, sipping a glass of white wine and standing back and looking, and seeing the way it all fit. The stuff I'd brought back from antique dealers in New Hampshire, the cookware, gleaming and virginal, that I had bought at Williams Sonoma, the things I had used to build a new life, art books, paintings, the nice set of useful tools in a neat metal tool box, that my father had given me when I moved in, all scattered among the broken shards of "good china" that my mother had offered, so I could entertain fashionably in my new place, even the very posed picture of herself that my annoying sister had given me. I had loved all of it. Too much, probably.

Richie had never cared much about stuff. But I did. I cared about the place I had made for myself, where I could be a detective, and be a painter, and be a woman, and be alone and take care of Rosie. The lousy bastards. Momentarily I had a passionate desire to call Richie. He'd fix it. But of course, I couldn't call Richie. After the momentary madness, I didn't even want to call Richie. I put my face down against Rosie's broad little back. She smelled good. I began to cry. She turned her head and lapped my cheeks. I didn't mind crying. This was where I was allowed to. My home. I could cry or get drunk, or make love, or be by myself, or do anything else I wanted with no one to approve or disapprove. I didn't need to call anyone. I was enough. I kept my face buried in Rosie's back, and my arms around her. After a time I didn't feel like crying any more.

"Well," I said to Rosie, "so they've burned Tara, the bastards. We can build it again."

Rosie wagged her tail. I got the cell phone out of my purse and called my insurance broker.

CHAPTER 37

John Otis called my new answering machine and left a message that if I wished to talk with him, he'd meet me in the lobby of New England Baptist Hospital. I arrived at the appointed time and sat down. There were half a dozen people in the lobby, including the woman at the information desk. New England Baptist specialized in orthopedics and a lot of people came and went on canes and crutches and walking casts. At about ten minutes past the hour, John Otis came in. It took me a moment to spot him without his white butler's coat. He looked carefully around the room before he walked over.

"Thanks for coming," he said. "My mother lives with my brother just down the hill, and I usually visit her on my day off."

"This is fine," I said.

"Can we go talk in the cafeteria," Otis said. "I haven't eaten."

We went down to the hospital cafeteria. I got some coffee and John Otis got a container of milk and a tuna sandwich.

"My mother always tries to feed me, but it's so unhealthy," he said. "Lot of fried stuff."

"Did Billie tell you why I wanted to talk with you?"

"About Millie," he said and smiled. "Millie and Billie. Sounds like a sitcom."

He sounded vaguely British. There was no hint of a black accent. Probably a condition of butlerhood.

"Billie says that man named Cathal Kragan came to the house."

"Yes."

"With another man."

"Once."

"You know the other man's name?"

John Otis was very neat. He ate his sandwich with small neat bites, dabbing at his lips neatly after every bite with a paper napkin. He drank his milk from the cardboard container with a straw.

"No. He only came once."

"When?"

"About a month ago."

"Do you remember the car that they came in?"

"Mr. Kragan, when he came, would normally drive a Dodge sedan. You know the funny cab forward kind."

"I've seen the ads. How about when he came with the other man?"

"Came in a limousine."

"Did you happen to get the license plate number?"

"Yes. Special license plate. Crowley-8."

"Crowley limos?"

"Yes, ma'am."

"The big Boston outfit."

"Yes, ma'am."

"Sunny. Please call me Sunny."

"The driver waited for them and drove them home."

"Did Kragan use a limo often?"

"No. Just that time."

"Did anybody else come in limos?"

Otis chewed his small bite of sandwich and swallowed and drank a small sip of milk through his straw and put the milk back down, and looked at me for a time without any expression. His eyes were black. His dark smooth face had no expression.

Finally he said, "Why do you ask?"

"It's all I could think of," I said.

"The women came in Crowley limousines."

"Women?"

"Mr. Patton would often entertain women," he said. "They always came in the same limo, Crowley-8. That's why I remember."

"Did Mrs. Patton join her husband," I said, "when he entertained these women?"

Otis's smooth face didn't change, but somehow I knew he was repressing a smile.

"Not that I know of."

We were quiet for a time. Otis finished his sandwich. Doctors and nurses and ambulatory patients and visitors passed us as we sat.

"My wife says you've promised not to reveal that we've talked to you."

"Not unless I must."

"No one would hire us if they thought we talked about our employer."

"So why take the risk?" I said.

"We feel badly for the little girl," he said.

CHAPTER 38

The insurance company had sent a clean-up team to my loft and while I was short some paintings, and there was no extra-virgin olive oil in the cupboards, and the good china hadn't been replaced yet, my home was livable again. Rosie and I were there, waiting for Brian Kelly. It was a business meeting, but he offered to bring Chinese food. I took a shower.

I was thoughtful about my underclothes. And I put clean sheets on the new bed.

Brian brought enough Chinese food to sustain the Ming dynasty for a year, and we ate it sitting at my counter. Rosie joined us. She could track Chinese food through a forest fire. I supplied some Gewürztraminer to go with the Chinese food, and we drank some while we ate and looked at a list of all homicides that had occurred in Massachusetts since the day Millicent heard her mother order someone killed. There were sixteen of them. Three appeared to be related. A man named Fitzgerald, a man named O'Neill, and a man named Ciccarelli.

"Somebody's trying to push into Boston, from the outside," Brian said. "So far it's Dagos 2, Micks 1."

"It doesn't sound like my case," I said.

Three deaths were women, so we eliminated them. We eliminated two because they were street gang killings, one because it was a murder-suicide. We eliminated two armored-car guards in Agawam who had been killed during a stickup. They'd taken one of the robbers with them. That left four that might be the one that Betty Patton had discussed.

"Of course the killing might not have happened in Massachusetts," Brian said.

"Do you have a national list?"

"No."

"Can you get one?"

"What do you think?" Brian said.

"I think it's one of those things that sounds simple and isn't."

Brian smiled.

"So let's go with the list we've got," I said.

"Better than nothing," Brian said. "You eat, I'll read them to you. Number one is Charles V. Powell, age forty-six, marketing director for the phone company, works in Boston, lives in Duxbury. Married, three kids, shot to death in the hall outside his girl-friend's apartment in Charles River Park. Murder weapon was a .38. Our guys think the wife did it. But nobody saw it and we can't find the gun. No residue on the wife's hands."

"She could have worn gloves," I said.

"I know. Everybody watches television. Number two is Kevin Humphries, a plumber, thirty-five years old, no kids, separated from his wife. Runs his own business in Fram-ingham. Shot while he was sitting in his car outside a restaurant on Route 9. Two bullets in the back of the head. Close range. Nine mm. Ex-wife's got an alibi. No suspects. Framingham cops think it was a hit."

"A plumber from Framingham might do work in South Natick," I said.

"If they could get him to show up," Brian said.

"I know," I said, "if he was my plumber I'd know why he was shot."

"Doesn't sound much like someone who'd be involved with Betty Patton though," Brian said.

"Maybe she liked guys with pipe dope on their hands."

"Number three is a political consultant.

197

Mason Blumenthal, forty-one, single, lived in the South End, shot in the chest three times with a .357. I was on that one. No leads, but I don't think he'd tickle Mrs. Patton's gonads."

"Gay?"

"Probably."

"Lover's quarrel?"

"Probably."

"Is there one more?"

Brian ate a mouthful of chicken with cashews and swallowed and drank some wine and then picked up the printout.

"Casper Willig," Brian read. "Forty-two years old, divorced, two kids, ran a photo supply store in Worcester. Lived alone in Shrewsbury. Found him in the trunk of his car parked in the garage at the Crown Plaza Hotel in Worcester. Two slugs in the forehead and three in the chest. Behind in his alimony. Behind in his child support. Maxed out on all his credit cards—he had seventeen."

"Jesus," I said.

"Seventeen. Looking at his credit situation, Worcester cops think he probably was behind to a loan shark."

"They kill you, they don't get their money," I said.

"So they don't like to kill you," Brian said. "I know. Maybe he was supposed to be an example for others."

With his chopsticks Brian handed a piece of beef in oyster sauce down to Rosie. She ate it carefully.

"If he weren't a plumber, I'd like the guy from Framingham," I said.

"You figure she was having an affair with someone?"

"There's the reference to what tingles her gonads," I said. "What would be your guess?"

"Affair." Brian said. "You think she's too snooty to have an affair with a plumber?"

"Snooty?" I said.

"Yeah. What's wrong with snooty?"

"I haven't heard anyone use that word since my grandmother died."

"So I'm an old-fashioned guy," Brian said.

"Well," I said. "She's very *snooty*. But, you know how some women are. If he's a hunk, the more working class the better."

"Like me," Brian said.

It was starting. I knew it would and now it had. I always loved the feeling in my stomach when it started. Even if he wasn't Richie.

"No need to be so self-effacing," I said.

"You too snooty to be interested in a cop?"

"You have anyone in mind?" I said.

"I was thinking about me," Brian said.

"Yes," I said. "So was I."

Brian leaned forward and kissed me. I closed my eyes. When I opened them he was off the barstool and standing beside me. Holding the kiss, I slid off my stool and we embraced. The kiss stopped. We leaned back against each other's arms and looked at each other. Rosie insinuated herself among our ankles and panted up at us.

"I know how she feels," Brian said.

"Does my breath smell of beef in oyster sauce?" I said.

"And you taste of Gewürztraminer," Brian said.

"A treat for all the senses," I said. "Perhaps I should ask Rosie to stay in the bathroom for a little while."

"Will she yowl?" Brian said.

"No, but I might," I said.

CHAPTER

39

The Framingham plumber was the best bet, so I started with him. A Framingham detective with gray hair and sideburns let me into Kevin Humphries' office in a storefront off Route 126. The detective's name was Bob Anderson. The office was two rooms. The front room was full of plumbing supplies and tools scattered around a yellow pine desk with a file drawer. The back room had a bed, and a bathroom, which looked as if Kevin had added it recently.

"He was apparently living here after the separation from his wife," Bob told me.

"Not well," I said.

"But quiet," Bob said. "I got seven kids."

"Well, Kevin won't be using the place anymore," I said.

"I know. His wife won't come near it. Says he was, excuse the language, a rotten prick when he was alive, and dying didn't change that. So here it sits like he left it, until something happens with his estate."

I nodded.

"I guess I'll nose around for a while," I said.

"I'm supposed to stay here while you do, but I could use some coffee."

"Go for it. I won't steal anything."

"We got a call from a Boston detective."

"Brian Kelly?"

"Yeah. Area C. Says you're working with him and he'll take responsibility for you."

"Brian's a sweetie," I said.

"Yeah," Bob smiled. "Me, too. I'll be over there in the coffee shop. Gimme a yell when you're through."

When he had left with visions of lemon-frosted scones dancing in his head, I went to the sloppy desk and opened the file drawers and took out the files. They were a series of manila folders with no designation on the tabs. The folders were bent and stained, and the work orders and receipts in them were not arranged in any order that I could recognize. I began to go through them. It was slow work. Many of the work orders were folded over, sometimes two or three times, as if they had been jammed into a shirt pocket. A lot of the paper made no sense to me. It referenced plumbing procedures or tools or supplies that I knew nothing of. But I could read the names on the slips and after an hour and a half, back nearly two years, I found a work order for Patton in South Natick. It appeared to be a matter of installing a full bath downstairs. It was marked paid in full.

Because I'm thorough, I went on back through the rest of Humphries' files. He kept them going three years back. There was nothing else that told me anything. But Mrs. Patton had agreed that a man should be killed. A man was killed and he had a connection to the Pattons. How big a coincidence was that? I went out of the office and closed the door and walked across the parking lot to the coffee shop. Anderson was having a piece of pie and some coffee at the counter.

"Something to eat?" he said.

I slipped onto a stool beside him.

"Tea," I said to the counter woman. "With lemon."

The woman nodded with the hint of contempt that counter people always show when you order tea.

"Maybe," I said. "Do you have any pictures of the plumber?"

"We got some nice crime scene shots," Anderson said.

"Swell," I said. "Always the best kind for identifying somebody."

"And we blew up a couple photos from his wedding."

"Can I get those?"

"Sure. What'd you find?"

"He did some plumbing work for a client of mine."

"You think the client might have had something to do with his death?"

"Maybe."

"Gimme a name."

I shook my head.

"Not yet," I said.

"I could put the question a little different," Bob said.

"I'll tell you as soon as I know something. Right now all I have is suspicion."

"I could still put the question a little different."

"Please give me some room," I said. "If it turns out there's a collar, I promise you'll get it."

Anderson didn't say anything.

"And I pay for the pie," I said.

"Bribing an officer?" he said.

"You bet," I said.

"Coffee, too," he said.

"Sure thing."

"Too rich to turn down," he said.

He took a card from his shirt pocket and gave it to me.

"You get something conclusive, you call me first."

"Unless I can't," I said.

"You don't bend a hell of a lot, do you?"

"No more than I have to," I said.

I gave him my most enticing smile. Nothing wrong with feminine wiles. Maybe I should bat my eyes.

40

I showed the pictures of Kevin Humphries to Millicent. It was a head-and-shoulders shot, a little grainy from being enlarged, but still clear enough for identification. He was wearing a gray tuxedo with black velvet lapels and a ruffled yellow tuxedo shirt with pearl studs. His hair was longish and his neck looked strong. Millicent wrinkled her nose.

"God, who's that?" she said.

"I was hoping you might recognize him," I said.

"Him? Ugh."

"Why 'ugh'?"

"He's such an Italian Stallion."

"I don't think he's Italian."

"Well you know, he's so *hey-let's-have-a-couple-brewski's.*"

"Low-class?"

"Yeah, and so macho man."

"How can you tell all that from the picture?"

"I don't know, I just can."

"Like an ink blot," I said.

"What?"

"You know, those tests where they show you an ink blot? Ask you what it looks like?"

She shook her head.

"Doesn't matter," I said. "I assume you don't know him."

"No. Am I supposed to?"

"He's a plumber," I said. "Worked once at your house."

"I don't pay any attention to plumbers," Millicent said.

"I was more wondering if your mother did."

"My mother? A plumber?"

Rosie had a half-chewed tennis ball which she was pushing around the floor in hopes that I might be inspired to throw it for her so she could chase it. She pushed it under the chair by my feet and looked at me. I sighed and picked it up and rolled it down the length of the loft. Rosie dashed after it, skidding on the rug by the television set as she went.

"I don't know how to say this, exactly, but I think it needs saying. You really probably can't make judgments about people by the way they look or what they do for a living or what country their ancestors came from."

"Huh?"

"You've grown up in circles that probably made such judgments all the time. Judgments about class, and income, and race, and religion, and work history. It's not your fault, but if you're going to outgrow your family you need to stop doing that."

"Well, I don't like macho men. Look at his neck."

"You like Spike, don't you?"

"He's not a macho man, he's gay."

"There you go again," I said.

"What?"

Rosie was back with her ball, dropping it on the floor in front of me and picking it up and dropping it.

"Throw the ball for Rosie," I said.

Millicent picked the ball up and fired it the length of the loft, a lot harder than she needed to, and Rosie was after it, scrambling, as the ball bounced around. I smiled. Millicent was annoyed. Excellent. Annoyed was so much better than disinterested.

CHAPTER 41

I was outside the Crowley Limousine dispatch office with Brian Kelly.

"This isn't even my case," Brian was saying to me.

"I know, but they'll never talk to me. I need somebody with a badge."

"If there's a crime it belongs to Framingham," Brian said.

"That may be," I said. "But did anyone in Framingham take you to paradise last night?"

"Well, no."

"Is anyone from Framingham going to do it again tonight?"

"I don't think so."

"Then?"

"Let's get in here," Brian said. "I've got a number of questions for the dispatcher."

The dispatcher was a large woman in a flowered ankle-length dress, the hem of which just brushed the tops of some blue-and-white Nike running shoes. "Mr. Patton is a very good customer," the dispatcher said. "I don't think he'd like us talking about his business."

"Yeah," Brian showed her his badge. "But I would."

She took the time to look closely at the badge, as if to make sure it didn't say Chicken Inspector on it.

"We're looking for a particular instance," I said. "Two men went out to see Mr. Patton in one of your limos. About a month ago."

If she thought by the "we" that I, too, was a Boston cop, no harm to it. The dispatcher stared at me a moment.

"Two men," she said.

"Un huh?"

"Last month?"

"About a month ago."

The dispatcher sat at the computer and manipulated the mouse.

"Got a trip on the fifteenth of August," she said.

"Tell us about it," I said.

Brian and his magic badge leaned against the filing cabinet beside her desk. She looked at him. He smiled at her.

"Pick up two men at an address in Swampscott. Take them to Mr. Patton's home in South Natick. Wait and return."

"What were the men's names?"

"Just one name, Mr. Kragan."

"Address?"

"Mr. Patton's."

"No, the pickup address in Swampscott."

"33 King's Beach Terrace."

"Who's the driver?"

"College kid, Ray Jourdan, lives on St. Paul Street in Brookline." She gave us the address. We left and got back in Brian's car and drove back to my loft. I got out. Brian got out and came around and stood next to me.

"I got to check in at the station," he said.

"I think I can take it from here," I said. "The driver will talk because his employer sent me."

"I don't think you should face Kragan alone."

"I'll have less chance to learn anything," I said, "if there's a Boston cop standing around."

"How about your ex-husband," Brian said. "Kragan might walk a little softer if he was around."

"He's baby-sitting Millicent," I said, "while Spike's working lunch."

"Everything we know about Kragan says he's dangerous," Brian said.

"Remember how we met," I said.

Brian put his arms around me.

"I remember," he said.

"So you know, I am not without resources."

"I know," Brian said.

We hugged each other for a moment. Then Brian pulled back a little and grinned down at me.

"In a pinch," he said, "you could probably love him to death."

I smiled, and said "You should know."

"Yeah," he said. "The voice of experience. Will I see you tonight?"

"I'll call you," I said.

Ray Jourdan lived on the second floor of a three-story walk-up off Washington Street. He was a light-skinned black man with merely the implication of an accent, which I guessed was Caribbean. He told me he was a graduate student at B.U.

"I always drove for Mr. Patton," he said.

"You ferry his girls back and forth."

"Girls?"

"When Mrs. Patton was out, Mr. Patton would have girls brought out to the house," I said. "They'd come in a limo. License tag says Crowley-8. You always drive for Patton..."

"Yes. I brought the girls."

"Where did you pick them up?"

"In the parking lot outside the Chestnut Hill Mall. Front entrance."

"Same girls each time?"

"I'm not sure."

"You can't tell one from another? Didn't you get out and hold the door?"

"They were always Asian," Ray said. "They tend to look alike to me."

"Well, aren't you politically incorrect."

Ray smiled. He was nervous about this, but he was contained.

"And me a minority myself," he said. "But it's true. I don't think they were the same girls, but I couldn't tell for sure."

"Did you deliver them back to the mall?"

"Yes."

"How long did they stay?"

"Usually I'd have them back to the mall about one-thirty, two o'clock in the morning."

"You just left them in an empty parking lot, in front of a closed mall?" I said.

"Yes, ma'am. Those were my instructions. The girls never said not to."

"Any idea how they got to and from the mall?"

"Maybe they lived around there," Ray said.

"In Chestnut Hill?"

"Well, just a thought."

"While the girls were at the house, were there other people there?"

"I don't know. I waited in the car."

"Were there other cars."

"No."

"When you took Cathal Kragan out, there was another man as well."

"Who?"

"Cathal Kragan, not a name you'd be likely to forget, is it?"

"No, no. I remember him."

"And the other man?"

"I don't know his full name. Mr. Kragan called him Albert."

"Anything else?"

"I think Albert might have been from Providence. They talked about some restaurants down there. You know, Al Forno? Places like that."

"Did they talk at all about Mr. Patton," I said. "Or Mrs. Patton?"

"No."

"You have no idea why they were visiting."

"No."

I thought about it for a while. Albert, from Providence.

"This is a good job for a guy needs to work part-time," Ray said. "Lot of time sitting and waiting, you can study. If you tell Mr. Patton you've been talking to me, I'm pretty sure he'll have me fired."

"I don't see why I'd have to tell him," I said.

"At least until I get my degree," Ray said.

CHAPTER 42

In Massachusetts, the record of political campaign contributions for all candidates is available to the public from the Secretary of State's office. With Millicent and Rosie in the car I parked illegally outside the statehouse. A cop came over. I rolled the window down just enough for Rosie to stick her head out and try to lap the cop.

"Lady," he said. "Can you read... Sunny darlin'!"

"Tommy, this is Rosie, and this is my friend Millicent. I just have to run in for a couple minutes."

Tommy Hannigan put his hand out and let Rosie lap it.

"Put yourself right there, darlin'," Tommy said. "Next to the Buick. Space is reserved for a guy shows up every year for the Christmas party."

"Good, Tommy. Can you keep an eye on my dog and my friend?"

"Certainly," he said. "How's your dad?"

"Just fine," I said. "You know he's retired."

"Two more years for me," Tommy said. "Take your time. I'll be right here till then."

I went in and got the list of political contributors for Brock Patton. I went back, gave Tommy a kiss, got in my car, and went on down the back of Beacon Hill to Cambridge Street. I parked at a hydrant outside the Starbucks on Cambridge, and went in and got two oatmeal maple scones and two cups of Guatemalan coffee. I brought them out, gave coffee and a scone to Millicent, and a half a scone to Rosie, and kept the other half for me.

"We going to sit here while you read that stuff?" Millicent said.

"Yep."

"What am I supposed to do?"

"Drink your coffee. Eat your scone. Give bites of it to Rosie. Watch the people passing by. Savor the moment of uncompromised leisure that you're afforded."

Millicent sighed loudly.

"Can I play the radio?" she said.

"Sure. Anything but talk radio. I can't stand talk radio."

She fiddled with the radio, moving irritably from one station that played hideous music to another station that played hideous music. Where's Neil Diamond when you need him.

I had just taken a bite of the scone and a short slurp of Guatemalan coffee, and Millicent had just tuned in her fifth hideous heavy metal station, when I came across the name Albert Antonioni, of Providence, Rhode Island. I was two names past it, someone named Amaral, when I stopped and went back. Albert, from Providence. That's what the driver had said about who was with Cathal Kragan in the back of the limo when they called on Brock Patton. I was orderly and patient. I went through the whole list, which took a second scone and trips for two more cups of coffee. There were other Alberts, and there were other people from Providence. But none that were both.

"Do you know anyone named Albert Antonioni?" I said to Millicent.

"No."

"He might have been a friend of your father's?"

"No."

She fiddled with the dial some more.

Albert Antonioni. The name seemed familiar. There was some kind of Italian movie guy named Antonioni, but the name was familiar in a different context.

"I have to make some calls," I said to Millicent.

She didn't react, so I reached over and turned the radio off.

"Just while I call," I said.

She slumped in the front seat and stared out the window. Rosie climbed around from the back seat and got in her lap. Before she could catch herself Millicent patted her. I picked up the car phone my mother had given me for Christmas last year, and made some phone calls and ended up talking to a detective in the Providence Police Intelligence unit named Kathy DeMarco.

"He's the man down here," Kathy told me. "When the old man died, and Junior went to jail, Antonioni was the guy who had to run things for the mob. At first it was temporary but pretty soon Albert was consolidating. And he consolidated the opposition right out of existence. And now he's the man."

"The usual way?" I said.

"Of consolidating? Yeah: bang, bang."

"Might he be expanding?" I said.

"Be his style," Kathy said.

"Is he connected at all to Brock Patton?" I said. "Who used to be the president of Roger Williams Trust?"

"Not that I know. Lemme bring it up on the screen."

I waited.

"Got nothing under Antonioni," Kathy said. "Lemme look under Patton."

I waited some more.

"No Brock Patton," Kathy said.

"How about Cathal Kragan?"

"Who?"

I spelled it.

"That his real name?"

214

"I don't know," I said. "Just a guy I'm trying to locate."

"What are we," Kathy said. "A dating service?"

"I don't want to date Cathal Kragan," I said.

Kathy looked it up.

"No Cathal Kragan," she said.

"Thank you," I said. "Can I get a picture of Antonioni?"

"Sure, Sunny, all part of the service," Kathy said.

"Actually," I said, "I know it isn't. So thank you."

"You're welcome," she said.

I gave her my address.

"If I come across the elusive Cathal," Kathy said, "I'll give you a buzz."

"Be sure it's the right Cathal Kragan," I said.

"I'll try to sort them out."

We hung up. I left it in the cradle and pushed the speakerphone button and called the answering machine in my loft. I pictured the empty loft with a new canvas sitting and waiting on the new easel. I felt displaced, drinking yuppie coffee with my yuppie cell phone listening to messages from my empty home.

There was a message from my mother saying that they were worried because I was never home when they called.

The next message said, "If you do not return Millicent Patton to her parents, you will be killed."

"It's him," Millicent said next to me.

"Who."

"The man in the bathroom that looked right at me. The man was with my mother, when you know... him."

I rewound the message and we listened again. The voice was deep and contemptuous and full of power.

"It's him," Millicent said again. "What are you going to do?"

"Let me just hear my messages," I said. "Then we'll talk."

The last message was from Anderson, the Framingham cop who had let me into Kevin Humphries' plumbing office.

"Got something you might be interested in," Anderson said. "Gimme a call."

I shut off the phone. And sat back and took a breath.

"Clues are pouring in," I said to Millicent.

"What you going to do about him? The man? He said he was going to kill you."

"I won't bring you back," I said. "If that's worrying you."

"No. I knew you wouldn't," Millicent said. "But he said he'd kill you."

"Actually he said I'd be killed."

"Whatever," Millicent said. "What are you going to do?"

"Sooner or later," I said, "I'm going to have to confront him."

"No."

"Yes."

"You can't. He'll kill you."

"I'll arrange it so he won't," I said.

"You know who he is."

"I believe he's a man named Cathal Kragan. I think he sent those men that came to our door. I believe he killed a man that I talked with named Bucko Meehan. And he might have killed a man in Framingham named Kevin Humphries."

"Don't go."

"I have to go," I said. "This is what I do."

"But what about me? What if he kills you?"

"I won't go yet," I said.

CHAPTER 43

On Thursday nights, I took an art history class at Boston University, and Julie had evening office hours for people who could see her at no other time. Afterward we would usually meet for a glass of wine somewhere in Harvard Square near Julie's office. Tonight we were at the bar in the new Harvest.

"I feel like all of a sudden I'm a mother," I said to Julie. "It's so exciting to be out by myself without Millicent."

"Is she with Spike?"

"No, Richie. Spike's working and Richie was coming by anyway to visit Rosie."

Julie nodded.

"Out and about," she said.

"You have real kids of your own." I said. "But you must feel that way sometimes."

"God yes," Julie said. "Anytime I'm away from them. Except of course when I'm feeling that way I'm also feeling guilty that I'm feeling that way."

"I know."

"I wonder if fathers feel that way?"

"Well," I said. "They have more of a tradition of being away from the kids, supporting them and all that."

"I know," Julie said, "But I swear Michael is a better mother than I am."

"Maybe he's just a good father," I said.

"He seems to want to be with them all the time. He likes to take them with us when we go places."

"Which makes you feel selfish and unloving," I said.

"You bet."

Julie finished her wine and gestured at the bartender for another glass."

"You love the kids," I said.

"Yes."

"And Michael loves them."

"Yes."

"That's all each of you can do," I said. "Love them the way you can."

"Sometimes I think it's easier if you don't love them."

"It's not," I said.

The bartender brought Julie her wine. Julie studied me for a moment before she picked up her glass and drank.

"This thing with Millicent is riding you, isn't it?" she said.

"Of course," I said.

"Want to talk about it?"

"I thought you'd never ask. I'm trying to save her and the only way I can is to solve the crime she's a part of, and I can't solve it if I'm taking care of her all the time. And I can't take the risks I would normally be willing to take, because all of a sudden I have to worry about her."

"You've always had to worry about Rosie," Julie said.

"Yes, but if something happened to me, Richie would take her and in a little while she'd be fine."

"Dogs are good that way."

"But who would take Millicent?" I said.

"She does have a mother and father," Julie said.

"She can't be with them," I said.

Julie stared at her wine. The bar was crowded. The two bartenders were busy.

"And Richie can't take her."

"No. Why would he? He barely knows her."

"That was true of you when you took her."

I didn't say anything.

"Wasn't it?" Julie said.

"There was no one else to do it," I said. "And it had to be done."

I had a second glass of wine. Julie had a third.

"Too bad you and Richie can't work it out," Julie said.

"Maybe we will," I said.

"Tell me again why you're not together?"

"Well for one thing he won't give up the family business."

"And neither will you," Julie said.

"Me?"

"How many people in your family have been cops?"

"Besides my father?"

"Un huh."

"Two uncles, and my grandfather."

"Un huh."

"I'm not a cop."

"Sure."

"Always a damned therapist," I said.

Julie was quiet.

"So maybe there's some fault on both sides," I said. "It still means that one of us needs to change to be with the other one."

"What's wrong with that?"

I shook my head.

"I can't think about that now," I said. "I have to figure out what to do with Millicent."

"How about private school?"

"Private school costs a lot of money."

"Maybe you can get money from the parents."

"I can't send her away now. She's in too much danger."

"Do you really think so?"

"I think when those men came to my door, they weren't trying to take her back to her parents. I think they were going to kill her."

"Because?"

"Because of what she saw," I said.

"The man with her mother?"

"Yes. There are some big-league players involved."

"And Richie can't help you?"

"I don't know if he can or can't. But I'm pretty sure he shouldn't."

"Because you're separated?"

"Yes. I won't live with him, won't sleep with him. But I can ask him to take care of me, help with anything I can't handle myself?"

"You talk as if sleeping with someone were a tradeoff for something else," Julie said.

"It just isn't right for me to have it both ways."

"What's Richie think?" Julie said.

"I don't know."

"Maybe you should ask him," she said.

CHAPTER 44

I was sitting with Bob Anderson in a frosted-glass cubicle in the detective unit in the Framingham Police Station.

"Humphries," Anderson was saying, "the plumber got killed on Route 9."

"Yes," I said.

"He had a mailbox at one of those private mail services, wife didn't know anything about it, except the bill came this month. And since he's not around to pay it, the wife gets it. Well, she says she's got no use for a private mailbox and she wants to cancel it and the service says fine, but you need to clean the box out. So she does and all she finds is this big fat envelope. And when she opens it she figures she better bring it to us, which she did, and I thought you might want to take a gander."

"I do," I said.

Anderson slid the envelope toward me. It was a big one, whatever the next bigger size is to 8 $\frac{1}{2}$ by 11. It was addressed to Kevin Humphries, care of the private mailbox service. It was full of pictures and the pictures were of Betty Patton and a man having sex. Having sex doesn't really do them justice. They were having every variety of sex mammals were capable of having. I looked at the pictures for a time, turned a couple of them upside down, or maybe right side up, I couldn't be sure.

"This is, I take it, the late Kevin Humphries," I said.

"Yep."

"You know the woman?" I said.

"Nope. You?"

I shook my head.

"Doesn't look anything like your client, does it?"

I shook my head again. Anderson shrugged.

"Who's seen these pictures," I said.

"Mrs. Humphries," Anderson said.

"And maybe a few guys in the station," I said.

"Maybe all the guys in the station," Anderson said.

"And nobody knows the woman?"

"That's what they say," Anderson said. "Just like you."

"Well," I said, "she gets credit for inventive, whoever she is."

"Yeah. The picture of them in the rocking chair, I'm not exactly sure what they're doing... you?"

"Well, not specifically," I said, "though I recognize the general, ah, thrust."

Anderson smiled.

"You know what I'm betting, Sunny?" he said.

"What?"

"I'm betting that you do know who that woman is, and sooner or later, when it suits with whatever you're working on, that you'll tell me."

"Really?" I said. "Could I have a copy of these pictures?"

"Sunny," Anderson said, "there's forty-one pictures there. Evidence in a murder case. You know I can't give you any."

"I only need one," I said.

Anderson nodded.

"I got to go wash my hands, Sunny. You better not even think of taking any of those pictures while I'm gone. 'Cause I got them counted."

"Okay," I said.

Anderson got up and walked out of his cubicle. I looked at the stack of photographs. They weren't Polaroids. They were good-quality color photographs. I counted them.

There were forty-two. I selected one that showed Betty Patton clearly and full face in a completely compromising pose. I put that picture in my purse and put the other forty-one back in the envelope, and crossed my legs and folded my hands in my lap. In a couple of minutes Anderson came back. He walked to his desk, picked up the envelope and counted the pictures.

"Forty-one," he said.

I nodded.

"Does anything about those pictures bother you?" I said.

Anderson grinned at me.

"Aside from that," I said.

"Like who took them?" Anderson said.

"Yes. If they were taking pictures of themselves wouldn't they set the camera up on a tripod and use some sort of timer or remote?"

"That's what people usually do."

"These pictures are taken from different angles at different distances," I said. "And some of them seem to have been taken seconds apart from different angles and distances."

"So maybe there's a third party," Anderson said.

We looked at each other. Neither of us seemed pleased with the image of a third party with a camera lurking just outside of every picture.

"I guess there would have to be," I said.

"You suppose Humphries kept that private mailbox for anything else?" Anderson said.

"Well, he wouldn't want his wife to see

these pictures," I said. "Did he get other mail there?"

"No."

"How about the handwriting on the envelope?"

"Wife says it's his. Our guy says it matches other samples of his handwriting."

"So he rented the box to hide these pictures," I said.

"Looks like."

"If it were just his wife why wouldn't he just hide them in his office? They were separated. She says that she never went there."

"Un huh."

"If the woman in the pictures had money these would be a good basis for blackmail."

"Your client got money?" Anderson said.

"On the other hand, the picture taker could use them for the same purpose."

"One wouldn't preclude the other," Anderson said.

" 'Preclude,' " I said. "Wow."

"Impressive, huh?"

"And accurate," I said. "One would not preclude the other."

"Still be nice to know who the photographer was."

"It couldn't hurt," I said.

"Too bad, I only got forty-one of those pictures," Anderson said. " 'Cause if the broad in the pictures turned out, just by a crazy chance, to be your client, and you had one of the pictures you might be able to use it for leverage."

I didn't say anything.

" 'Course you gotta wonder," Anderson said, "would a woman who'd pose for pictures like this care about being blackmailed?"

"Maybe her husband would."

"Or maybe it's just vanity," Anderson said. "Maybe she told everyone she was a real blond."

CHAPTER 45

I was going to find something that Millicent liked to do if I had to invent a new pastime. Which was why we were sitting on two Alden fiberglass rowing shells, side by side on the river, twenty yards from shore, with a cold wind blowing at us.

"Have you ever rowed a boat?" I said.

"No."

Millicent was trying so desperately to balance that she could barely speak.

"Good," I said. "This is nothing like that, and if you had you'd just have to unlearn it."

Millicent said "yes" as minimally as possible. She looked entirely miserable in her yellow life vest.

"Okay, first, just let the oars rest on the water... That's right... Now rock the boat. Go ahead. See how long the oars are? You can't tip over with the oars spread like that."

Millicent shifted her weight a millimeter. The shell didn't tip.

"Good, now we'll just sit here a bit until you get used to it. We have as much time as we need. There's no reason to hurry."

We sat. It was early October and everything along the river near the boat club was still green. Cars moved steadily along the parkways on both sides of the river. People ran along the sidewalks next to the river, running the loop around the upper Charles where it bent toward Watertown, using the Larz Anderson Bridge to cross the river in one direction and the Eliot Bridge to cross in the other. We stayed in close to shore, out of the current, just far enough from land to keep the oars from hitting.

"Okay," I said, "see, you're not going to tip over."

"Yet," Millicent said between her teeth.

"Now, when you row, you want the blades to dip in, but not too deep, and of course to come out of the water entirely, but not too high. Watch me."

I rowed across the river and back staying where she could see me without turning. I remembered when I had first learned to row these boats. It was like sitting on a needle. I knew she wouldn't turn.

"Okay, now look at my hands, see how they are? It's all in the way you roll your wrist. See? Again. See?"

Millicent nodded very carefully, her head barely moving.

"Now you do it," I said.

"Where shall I row?"

"Just roll your wrists first, see how the blades turn?"

She tried it, rolling her wrists maybe a half an inch.

"Let's practice rolling the wrists so that the oar blades are vertical, then horizontal, vertical, horizontal, that's right. If you feel like you're losing your balance just let the oars drop onto the water, there, yes, like that."

We practiced that for a while. I wasn't having a nice time. I had housebroken Rosie faster than I was teaching Millicent to row. But it was the first thing she'd shown any interest in. She'd seen the college teams rowing on the river and said that it looked like it might be nice. I had pounced on it like an Ocelot. *I used to row,* I said, *in college.* She said, *Really?* I said, *Yes.* She said, *Could you teach me.* And here we were.

"It's the legs," I said, "that do the real work in rowing. You get the push off the big quadriceps. It's why the seat is like that. See, you lay out over the oars like this and then pull them toward you while you drive with your legs."

I demonstrated and my rental shell shot halfway across the river. I returned to her, back-stroking, stern first.

"You can try that now. Look around and make sure it's clear because the first stroke will send you a pretty good distance."

She did as I told her and caught a crab

228

with her right oar and almost fell out of the boat.

"Oars in the water," I said. "Oars in the water."

She did what I told her. The boat steadied. I looked at her. Her face was gray with fear and concentration.

"Everybody almost falls in," I said. "Try it again. Remember about rolling the wrists."

The gun at the small of my back was not appropriate to single-shell rowing, and I felt like we were two ducks sitting out there on the river in plain view. But I was goddamned if I was going to let Cathal Kragan bury us alive. And I was pretty sure he wouldn't be looking for us out on the river.

"Okay," I said, "I'll be right beside you, go ahead, don't press, let the oars into the water pull, extend your legs, good, roll the wrists, good."

We slid out across the dark water.

"Again," I said, "pull, push with the quads, roll wrists, relax. Try it with your eyes closed so that you get the full feel."

I felt like a single mother. It was too much to try and bring Millicent up and protect her and find the guys who wanted to kill her and figure out what was going on with her parents. I needed help and much of the help I needed was the kind that men usually were better at than women. The kind that Julie couldn't really give. The kind that Spike was good at, but how fair was it to ask him? The kind that Brian Kelly could give me, but he was a cop.

He had his own agenda. My father? *Daddy, I'm grown up and on my own but could you help me do my job?* Richie? *No, I won't sleep with you, but could you risk your life for me?* Did getting help mean selling out? I didn't mind getting help from Julie. Why was I having the vapors about getting a different kind of help from men? I was getting really sick of I-am-woman-hear-me-roar. Maybe if you're really integrated, you asked for the help you needed and got it on your own terms.

"Sunny," Millicent said as we sat side by side in the middle of the river and let the shells drift, "I'm sick of this. I want to go home."

Like that.

CHAPTER 46

Millicent was wearing an oversized bathrobe and drinking hot chocolate at Spike's kitchen table. The sleeves of the robe were turned up. Her hair was fluffed from the shower and she smelled of soap and shampoo and looked maybe twelve. Rosie sat on the floor beside her feet, looking up with her mouth open and her tongue lolling. If I didn't know better than to anthropomorphize dogs, I'd have said Rosie was smiling at Millicent.

"Did you like the rowing?" I said.

"It's awfully hard," she said.

She rubbed Rosie's chest absently with the toe of her right foot.

"I know, but it's sort of like riding a bicycle. Once you get the balance, it's not so hard."

"I know, I could feel that."

"Do you think you'll want to do it again?"

"Yes."

I was quiet. Millicent drank some hot chocolate.

"Your mother was having an affair with the plumber," I said.

"The plumber?"

"Yes, the one you said looked like an Italian Stallion."

"Him?"

"Yes."

"Are you sure? My mother? Did he tell you that?"

"I found pictures of them."

"Pictures?"

"Yes."

"You mean, dirty pictures? Like I found?"

"Yes."

"Jesus. It's like she sees a camera she yanks off her clothes."

"Some people like to pose," I said.

"With plumbers?"

"Sometimes what seems a drawback to one person seems an asset to another."

"What do you mean?"

"Maybe his being a working-class guy was his appeal."

"Well, it's sick," Millicent said.

"Yes," I said. "It probably is."

I took a deep breath. "We're never going to get to where we need to go," I said. "If you can't trust me to tell you the truth... The plumber was shot to death."

"Shot? You mean murdered?"

"Yes."

"Do you think it was my mother?"

"It happened after she talked with Cathal Kragan about somebody who would have to be killed."

"But there must have been a bunch of people killed since then."

"Sixteen," I said. "In Massachusetts. He's the only one we can connect to your mother."

Millicent looked at me without saying anything for a moment. The red smudges faded. She shrugged.

"Well, fuck her," she said. "I hate her anyway."

God, was I in over my head. I took in some more air. Rosie heard me and gave me a look. I smiled at her. It had been simpler when she was all I had to worry about.

"Yes," I said. "You probably do. And I don't see why you shouldn't. But you probably feel other things, too."

"Like what?"

"Loneliness, rejection, disappointment, fear."

"I don't feel anything," she said. "I'm fine."

"Sort of like when you were having sex with strangers in the backseat of a car," I said.

"Hey, I did what I had to do."

"I know. And because you had to, you tended to close down all your feelings so it wouldn't seem so awful. I'm not a shrink. I can't deal with that part of you, all I'm saying is don't close down on this."

She shrugged.

"When this is over..." I said.

"What?"

"This situation. When we've solved these problems and don't have to hide out here with Spike, I'm going to ask you to see a good psychiatrist."

"I already did that with Marguerite."

"No. I mean a real one that knows what he or she is doing."

"You don't think Marguerite knew what she was doing?"

"No," I said. "I don't."

"How do you know?"

"I talked with her. I believe she's a fraud."

"Oh, they're all frauds anyway, aren't they?"

"No. My friend Julie is a therapist."

"You want me to see her?"

"No. She'd be the first to tell you she wasn't right for you. But she can find us someone."

"You think I'm crazy?"

"I think you've had more to handle than a kid can handle alone. Hell, that anyone could handle alone. You need somebody to help you with it."

"You're helping me."

"Yes, but unlike Marguerite, I know my limitations."

"I don't want anyone else."

"We don't have to deal with it now, but when this is over you are going to need somebody else."

"Instead of you?"

Whoops. Of course she's scared. I should have foreseen it.

"No, not instead, in addition to. I'm permanent."

Rosie got impatient on the floor by Millicent's feet, and jumped up and put her forepaws in Millicent's lap and scanned the table for food. Still looking at me, Millicent patted Rosie's head. I could see the tears form in Millicent's eyes, then she put her head down against Rosie's and put her arms around Rosie and stayed that way while she waited for the tears to clear. I didn't say anything. Rosie didn't quite get the deal. She was still glancing sidelong at the table, her tail wagging, submitting graciously, but with no great pleasure, to the tears and the embrace.

CHAPTER 47

Brian Kelly had a three-story brick town house on First Street in South Boston. We were sitting together in postcoital languor, on the couch in his narrow, bow-windowed front room, with a fire in the small fireplace, and some red wine, talking business. I wore one of Brian's shirts, which came about to my knees. Brian was wearing tartan plaid boxers. We were both barefoot.

"Here's what I think I know," I said.

"And think you can can prove?" Brian said.

"Don't be so picky," I said. "I know that Betty Patton was having sex with the plumber, Kevin Humphries, who had been doing some work for them."

"How come that never happens to cops," Brian said.

"It does."

"Oh, you and me?"

"Exactly," I said.

"I know Betty posed for very explicit pictures of her relationship with Kevin, and I assume that he got hold of the pictures and blackmailed her with them. She told Kragan, and Kragan killed Humphries."

"You've seen the pictures," Brian said.

"Un huh."

"And you have the kid's testimony on the conversation she overheard between her mother and Kragan."

"Un huh."

"We know the guy she saw with her mother is Kragan."

"Pretty likely."

"Pretty likely? I can't wait to go in an tell some assistant DA that it's 'pretty likely.' "

"So don't, wait until I get more."

Brian leaned forward and poured a little more wine into each of our glasses.

"I know that Brock Patton is running for governor, and that a big campaign contributor is Albert Antonioni from Rhode Island. Do you know him?"

"I know Antonioni," Brian said.

"So I figure that if these pictures surfaced, the Patton gubernatorial campaign would suffer a setback."

"Depends how the First Lady looks in the buff," Brian said.

"Would you like to see the pictures?"

"You bet."

"Because they're evidence?"

"Sure."

"Men," I said.

Brian smiled.

"Antonioni is not backing somebody for governor of Massachusetts because he's concerned with good government," Brian said.

"True."

"He's investing in something that will pay off in the long term."

"It would be in anyone's interest to own the governor," I said.

"Especially if you're trying to reestablish an Italian presence among the wiseguys in Boston."

"Which somebody is," I said.

"Yeah. There's already been some skirmishing," Brian said. "The micks and the dagos. OCU says the dagos are from Providence."

"Except for Cathal Kragan."

"He's not from Providence?"

"He lives in Swampscott, and Cathal Kragan is an Irish name."

"Hire a guy knows the turf, I guess." Brian said.

"Whatever," I said. "There's a good motive in the connection between Patton, Kragan, and Antonioni."

"You know they're connected."

"I have testimony that Kragan and Antonioni came to Patton's house together," I said.

Brian was quiet for a time. We had our feet up on the coffee table. And we both stared into the fire while he was being quiet.

"There's one crime here," he said after a while. "The murder of Kevin Humphries. And you can't tie Kragan to it, or Antonioni."

"No," I said. "I can't. There is the matter of two men coming to my house and trying to kill me."

"You can't tie Kragan to that either," Brian said. "Only thing we had was testimony from Bucko Meehan, and he's dead."

"True."

"So you know a lot, but you can't prove much."

"Yet," I said.

"And the murder of the plumber isn't even in my district."

"Also true."

"We need to think about all of this," Brian said.

His arm was around me. I had pushed tightly in against him, with my head on his chest.

"What should we do while we're thinking?" I said.

"Hell, Sunny, I don't know."

"Maybe we should have sex again," I said.

"Why didn't I think of that," he said, and put his hand under the tail of the borrowed shirt. Our conversation was somewhat more exclamatory for a while, and then we were quiet and after a while we were still and I had his shirt back on, and the couch was back together, and he was pouring us some more wine. In the fireplace, the fire settled in on itself. I looked around the high-ceilinged nineteenth-century room.

"This is a very comfy house," I said.

"A remnant of my marriage," he said to me.

"Are there any others?" I said.

"Like kids? No. She took off with the man of her dreams before we ever got to kids."

"Does it still bother you?" I said.

He shook his head.

"The other guy thing bothered me for a while, but when I got over that I realized I was lucky to be rid of her."

"Is she still with the other guy?"

Brian laughed.

"She's gone through three more men of her dreams," he said. "Since then. I don't know how many of them she married."

"Has there been anyone since?" I said.

"For me?"

"Yes."

"One every Saturday night," Brian said. "None serious before now."

"Now?"

"Yeah."

"I don't know how serious this one ought to be," I said.

"You're not available?"

"I'm divorced," I said. "I'm available for this. But I don't know if I'm available for more than this."

"Why not?"

"I don't know if I'm really free of my ex-husband."

"I could help you get free," Brian said. "If he's giving you trouble."

"No. Richie is very decent about things. I don't know if I'm emotionally free of him. I don't even know if I want to be."

"So why'd you get divorced? His idea?"

"No. I left him."

"Because?"

"Do you know who my ex-husband is?"

"I know who his father is, and his uncles. That the reason?"

"One of them."

"He wouldn't give it up for you?"

"No."

"I would have."

"Would you?"

"Absolutely."

"Would you stop being a cop?"

"Yes."

"And be what?"

Brian started to speak and stopped and thought about it. As he thought about it he began to nod slowly.

"That's the question, isn't it," he said finally.

"Richie was never able to answer it," I said. "I'm not sure I gave him enough time."

"And be what," Brian said softly. "That your only issue?"

"No. I always felt as if I were being squeezed to death."

"That's never fun," Brian said. "My ploy would be probably not to do that."

I smiled and put my head on his chest again.

"Yes. That would be the right ploy," I said.

We were quiet. Brian smelled of soap and cologne, and a hint of new perspiration after a vigorous evening. The fire was quiet in the narrow fireplace. I stared at it. All of a sudden I found myself saying something that I hadn't known until I said it.

"If I can work it out so that I can be with Richie," I murmured, "I will."

I felt Brian stiffen a little. But he didn't pull away. I felt his hand pat my shoulder lightly.

"We'll see," he said as he patted. "We'll have to see."

CHAPTER 48

Rosie and I were in one of Rosie's favorite spots, a bench beside the swan boat lagoon in the Boston Public Garden. It was kind of late in the fall for sitting on a bench outside, but they hadn't drained the lagoon for winter yet, or put the swan boats away. Rosie could make eye contact with a dozen squirrels, and at least that many ducks, and not have to risk actually attacking them because she was on her leash. I liked to sit there when I felt stifled by things, as I did today. There was something about being outside in the sunlight with the dog that made my head clear. Rosie sat beside me. I had her leash looped over my wrist, but she seemed perfectly content leaning against me and focusing on the wildlife, her head moving fractionally as the squirrels hopped and the ducks glided, through whatever field of vision her black watermelon-seed eyes provided.

Brian was no more. He hadn't said it, and I hadn't. But I knew. He might be around for a time, if I changed my mind, but Brian's interests would be directed elsewhere. Which was healthy of him. I remembered the moment with Richie, too.

It was Julie's night out every Thursday. Michael took the kids, and Julie and I and sometimes Spike, on the rare occasion when our plans appealed to him, would go to an art exhibit or a book signing or maybe a musical evening at the Longy School in Cambridge, stuff that I found mostly boring, and Spike usually found insufferable, but stuff which reassured Julie that she was still an intellectual who had not been lobotomized by marriage and children. It was Spike's view that this grim dedication to what he called intellectual boot camp would lobotomize us all, but though less often than I, he went with her because, less

241

intensely than I, he loved Julie. This night, after a particularly grueling poetry reading in the basement of a church in the Back Bay, the three of us went to the Ritz bar and ordered martinis as an antidote to the stale cheese and warm white wine we had desperately ingested at the church. The relief we all felt was nearly tactile, though Julie wouldn't admit it, and we didn't press the point because we were kind. But the martinis went down really well, and the sum of it was that I came home to find Richie standing in the driveway with the dog's leash in his hands. The dog was inside. To this day I don't remember why he had it.

"Where have you been," Richie said.

As he spoke, he snapped the dog's leash tight between his hands and let it loose and snapped it tight.

"Out with my friends," I said.

"You're supposed to be home here with me," he said.

The leash snapped tight and loosened. I doubt that Richie was even aware of what he was doing. He was ferociously contained and when he was very angry it squeezed out around his containment in odd ways.

"Every minute?" I said.

Snap.

"I've been waiting for three hours."

The leash snapped. Did he want to snap it around my neck? No. Richie would never hurt me.

"I have the right," I said, in the dignified way that you can achieve only if you're drunk, "to be with my friends when I want to be."

242

"And I have the right to have you come home when you're expected and not make me think about whether it's time to call the cops or not."

"Oh, don't be so silly," I said.

"To worry about you is silly?"

"I can take care of myself."

"To want you with me is silly?"

"No. But if you do it too much it's..." I couldn't think of a word... then it came... "suffocating."

Richie stretched the leash as tight as he could, as if he were trying to pull it apart.

"Suffocating? Loving you and wanting you with me is suffocating?"

Had I been sober, maybe I would have modified it. It wasn't quite what I meant. But it never is in fights like that. And I wasn't sober.

"Yes!"

Richie shook his head like a horse beset by flies.

"All I ask is that I may love you and you love me back."

"And you define love, and you judge the terms in which I love you back? And if I don't love you in the same way you think you love me, I get yelled at?"

"I'm talking about the way I feel," Richie said.

"And I'm talking about the way I feel. Why do we have to feel exactly alike? Why can't you feel your way, and I feel my way?"

"All I want is to be loved the way I love," Richie said. He was snapping the leash again.

"Well, maybe you can't have that."

"That's what marriage is," he said.

"Maybe you married the wrong woman, then."

"Yeah," Richie said, "maybe I did."

Still holding the leash he walked away from me down the driveway and disappeared into the dark. When he came back I was in bed, and I pretended to be asleep.

Beside me, Rosie spotted another dog on the other side of the lagoon, and jumped down barking and snarling and gargling, just as if she would really attack it if I let her, which she wouldn't. But it was a dazzling display, and several pedestrians stepped hurriedly out of her way as she strained on the leash.

"At least I know you don't want to strangle me with it," I said, and got up and steered her back toward Boylston Street.

CHAPTER 49

Richie and Spike had never been easy with each other. The only thing they had in common was me. So it was a little strained around Spike's kitchen table a little after midnight. Millicent was in the den watching television. Rosie was on the floor between me and Richie, with her head resting on my left foot. There was fruit and cheese and some crackers and some wine on the table.

"You keep some tough hours, Sunny," Richie said.

He put a small wedge of blue cheese on each of two crackers, fed one to Rosie and ate the other.

"It's the only time I could get us all together," I said.

"Why do you want to?" Spike said.

"Because I need help."

"What've you been getting?" Spike said, "We've gone to the mattresses in my house, we're baby-sitting your client."

"I know. I'm grateful."

"Good," Spike said.

"What do you need?" Richie said.

"There's a man named Cathal Kragan," I said. "You know about him."

They both nodded.

"There's a man named Albert Antonioni. Do you know about him?"

"Not the Italian director," Spike said.

"No."

"From Providence?" Richie said.

"Yes."

"We know him."

"What's that," Spike said, "the royal *we?*"

Almost everybody who meets Richie is intimidated by him. It isn't size, though he's big enough; it's something in his eyes, and his voice, and how still he is when there's no reason to move. But Richie didn't intimidate Spike. As far as I knew nothing intimidated Spike, including things that should have.

"*We* always means his father and his uncle," I said.

Richie grinned. "Thank you for inter-
preting," he said. "Tell me about Antonioni."

I did. When I was through Richie and Spike
were both silent for a time. Richie poured a
little wine into my glass, and a little into his
own. He started to put the wine bottle down
when Spike said, "Hey."

Richie grinned and poured some into Spike's
glass. Spike nodded and raised the glass half an
inch in Richie's direction and drank some wine.

"You're right," Spike said to me when he
put the glass down. "You need help."

"And I don't know if I have the right to ask
for it," I said.

"Because?"

"Well, how much can you ask a friend to do?"
I said.

"You and I are more than friends," Richie
said.

"I know, that's an even bigger problem.
How can I ask you to help me, when we're...
when I'm not..."

Richie glanced briefly at Spike, and then took
in a little air.

"Sunny," he said. "There's nothing about
rights here. You need something from me, you
get it, whether you're sleeping with me or not."

My eyes stung. Horror of horrors, was I
going to cry? I breathed slowly.

"Thank you."

"You're welcome," Richie said.

A slow smile developed as he looked at me.

"Of course, afterwards," he said, "if you were
grateful..."

I sighed and looked at Spike.

"I'll help, too," he said, "and you won't have to sleep with me either."

"Easy for you..." Richie murmured.

Spike grinned.

"Just going along with the program," he said.

Richie cut a wedge from a Granny Smith apple and ate it and drank some wine.

"First off," Richie said, "what's your goal?"

"I've been sort of making it up as I went along," I said. "I'm not sure I've set a goal."

"Well, let's set one," Richie said.

"Saving Millicent," I said.

"From?"

"From Kragan, from Antonioni, if he's part of it, from her parents, from herself."

"The full bore, all out, hundred and ten percent save," Spike said. "Save her from everything."

"If I can."

"Would the first step be to take out the people who are trying to kill her?"

"Yes," I said, "and maybe, find out along the way if her parents are as bad as they seem."

"You assume they want to kill her because Kragan knows she overheard him and her mother planning to kill a guy."

"Yes."

"And because it would lead, if she talked, maybe to implicating Kragan and Antonioni and their participation in her father's gubernatorial ambitions," Richie said.

"Yes."

"So if we remove the motive, we remove the threat to the kid," Spike said.

"What would you like to do, Sunny?"

"I'd like to blow the whole thing out of the water," I said. "The sex, the murder, Patton's run for governor, Antonioni, Kragan, all of it. Boom!"

Richie nodded slowly. He looked at Spike.

"How good are you," he said.

Spike grinned at him. "About as good as you," he said.

"That's very good," Richie said.

"I know."

Richie looked at him some more.

"You want him in?" Richie said to me, staring at Spike.

"I trust him like I trust you," I said.

"Well," Richie said, "he's got the build for it."

"How sweet of you to notice," Spike said.

"One rule," Richie said, and he started to grin sooner than he wanted to. "There'll be no kissing."

Spike held his look for a minute and then he, too, began to smile.

"Damn," Spike said.

Richie looked at me. Then at Spike. Than back at me. He raised his glass. We raised ours.

"Boom!" he said.

CHAPTER 50

There was an exhibit of Low Country realists at the Museum of Fine Arts, and, on the assumption that Kragan's button men didn't normally hang out there, I took Millicent to see it.

"Why do I want to look at windmills and cows and people dressed funny?" Millicent said.

"I don't know," I said.

"But I mean, why would you? Why would anyone?"

"I like to look at them," I said.

"Why? Look at this picture of this woman, why is that better than a photograph?"

It was a painting by Vermeer.

"Sometimes I like to look at photographs, too," I said.

"You know what I mean."

"Yes," I said, "I do. For a minute there I was doing my grown-up shtick. Avoiding the question by sounding wise."

Millicent smiled.

"You didn't sound so wise to me," she said.

"But I was successfully avoiding the question."

" 'Cause you don't know the answer?"

I laughed.

"You know your grown-ups, don't you."

Millicent sensed an advantage and bored in.

"So why do you like this stuff," she said. "Because you're supposed to?"

"No, I'm past doing things because I'm supposed to. I like it. I like the way the painting seems so luminescent. I like the tranquility, I like the way the thing lays out, everything so balanced—space and containment. I like the expression on the woman's face, the details of the room."

"You could get that in a photograph."

"Well, not of this woman," I said. "It was done in the seventeenth century; they didn't have photographs."

"So this would be the only kinds of pictures there were."

"That's right," I said. "The only way they had to fix anything in time, so to speak."

"I don't even know what that means."

"Well, one of the reasons to look at stuff is to learn what things mean."

"I don't have to like stuff I don't like."

"No," I said, "you don't. But it's probably better to base your reaction on knowledge than on ignorance."

"What difference does it make? Whether I like it or not?"

"The more things you like, the more opportunities to be happy."

By now we were sitting on a little bench, and so intent on our conversation that we had stopped looking at the paintings.

"Okay," Millicent said, "that's what I asked you before. Why should I like that picture?"

"There's no should here. I am pleased by

how well Vermeer did what he did. But if you're not, once you've looked at it thoughtfully, then you're not."

"Well, you're a painter, so maybe it means more to you."

"Probably does. But I'm also pleased when I see old films of Ray Robinson, or listen to Charlie Parker, or read Emily Dickinson."

"I don't know who any of those people are."

"Yet," I said, "but now you know who Vermeer is."

Millicent shrugged. We sat for another moment, looking at the painting.

"You love Richie?" Millicent said.

"Jesus," I said, "what is this, your morning for impossible questions?"

"Well, either you do or you don't," Millicent said. "What's so hard about that?"

"I do," I said, "I guess."

"You act like you do," Millicent said. "You and him ever have sex?"

"Since the divorce?"

"Yeah?"

"No."

"How come?" Millicent said.

"It sends the wrong message, I think."

"But you'd like to?"

I could feel myself blushing.

"I don't know why, but this is embarrassing me," I said.

Millicent smiled happily.

"So you're not so perfect."

"Ain't that the truth," I said.

"You having sex with that cop?"

"Brian?" I said.

"Yeah, Brian whatsisname."

I felt myself blushing more. It was annoying. Why didn't I want to talk about this?

"I guess that's between me and Brian," I said.

"How come you won't tell me?"

"I don't know. I don't want to."

Millicent was radiant with triumph.

"You're always asking me stuff," she said.

I took in some air.

"I have never slept with anyone I didn't care for," I said. "Like most adults I have sex with people I do care for."

"So you care for Brian the cop?"

"Yes, I do."

"So... ?"

I smiled.

"You won't allow me my modesty, will you."

"You have had sex with him."

"I guess you've got me," I said.

Millicent was still intense.

"Say so," she said.

"Yes, I have," I said.

Millicent looked relieved. The tension went out of her shoulders. I felt like there had been a test. I wondered if I'd passed. Did she need to know I'd tell her everything? Was she trying to take me down a peg? I felt as if I needed another take on this conversation, as if I had botched most of my lines on the first take. But it was over, and the quality of satisfied closure in Millicent let me know that going over the same ground wouldn't do her any good. I'd noticed in the last few years that getting it said just right didn't do much for anybody but the sayer. What she had gotten was my genuine reaction. Revision wouldn't help. Help with what? I wished some sort of supershrink would leap out of a phone booth and explain to me just what the hell was going on. But none did. They never do. The bastards.

CHAPTER 51

I drove out to see Betty Patton through a much-too-early snowfall. The snow was accumulating on soft surfaces and melting as it hit the roadway. The streets were therefore wet and shiny as I wound through the west of Boston boondocks, and the lawns gleamed whitely. It wouldn't last long; this kind of snowfall never did, and its transience was probably part of why it was so pretty.

I had already checked with Brock Patton's office at the bank. He was there, though, of course, in a meeting where he was deciding the course of Western civilization, and could not be interrupted. I didn't mind. I just wanted to be sure I could talk to Betty Patton without him. John Otis opened the front door for me as formally as if I had never had a tuna sandwich with him on Parker Hill. He turned me over to Billie who was just as formal, and she led me down the hallway to a conservatory at the back of the house. Apparently the library, where I'd been before, was Brock's domain. Betty Patton rose from her little writing desk when I came in and walked toward me stiffly to shake hands. Billie left us.

"Please sit down, Miss Randall," Betty said.

I did. The floor of the conservatory was stone and I could feel the heat radiating gently up from it. Outside the glass walls, the light snow fell straight down, onto the long meadow that sloped down to the river. The room was furnished with sort of fancy garden furniture as if to emphasize the connection between the room and the out-of-doors. There were a lot of plants around. Since the only thing I know about plants is a dozen yellow roses, I didn't know what kind they were, but they seemed to be flourishing.

Betty Patton returned to her writing desk and sat and half turned in her chair to face me. She sat very straight, her hands folded in her lap. Her hair was perfect. Her makeup was flawless. She wore a Polo warm-up suit, in which, I suspected, no one had ever warmed up in the history of fashion.

"You may as well know, up front, Miss Randall," she said, "that our attorneys are preparing legal action against you for the return of our daughter. You stand an excellent chance of being charged with kidnapping."

"I'm all atremble," I said.

I took the embarrassing picture of Betty Patton from my purse and leaned over and placed it on the writing desk face up. She looked at it. And looked quickly away. Her face colored slowly until it was a full blush. Good. She was human. After a moment, she turned the picture over very slowly and placed it facedown on the desk. The snow fell straight down some more outside the glass walls. The heat continued to rise gently from the stone floor. Betty Patton stared at the blank white back of the photograph. She looked out the window. She looked past me at the door I'd come in. She looked back down at the face-down picture.

"Many people allow themselves to be photographed naked," she said.

I didn't say anything.

"Admittedly this is perhaps a bit beyond simple nakedness," Betty said.

I waited.

"I have needs," she said. "Sometimes I can't help myself."

I nodded.

"If you knew what being married to him was like," she said.

"You're not married to the man in the picture," I said.

"Of course not. I was referring to Brock."

I knew that, but I didn't comment.

"The man in the picture is a plumber," I said, "named Kevin Humphries. He did some work for you once. He's dead."

255

She continued to stare down at the back of the photograph. Then she looked up and her gaze was pretty steady.

"What do you want?" she said.

"This picture is just a sample. There are more."

She nodded.

"Tell me about him," I said.

"The plumber?"

"Yes."

"Why?"

"Because I want to know," I said.

"And you think you can threaten me with the pictures?"

"Yes."

"He came a year or so ago to put in a bathroom in my part of the house, off my bedroom."

"You and your husband had separate bedrooms."

"Yes. It had nothing to do with intimacy, it's just a matter of each of us needing more privacy."

"Sure," I said. "You were intimate."

"Of course, if it's any of your business."

"Someday I'll figure out what my business is," I said. "How did he get from plumber to lover?"

"Lover," Betty Patton said. "How quaint."

"It seemed so much more ladylike than 'fucker,' " I said.

"But the latter is far more accurate," Betty Patton said, and smiled.

At least the corners of her lips moved up. I think she intended it to be a smile. It was awful.

"He was a big, strong man, attractive in a sweaty, capable way, and I could tell he was interested."

I nodded again.

"I... as I said, I have needs."

"And the pictures?"

"I gave them to him. I wanted him to remember what we'd had."

"Did it occur to you that it might give him some leverage on you?" I said.

"I thought we mattered too much to each other. When it became apparent that we could no longer be together, I wanted him to have something that spoke to him of our intimacy."

"What made you break up?"

Betty Patton looked at me as if I were far too stupid to get in out of the rain.

"I am a married woman, if you hadn't noticed," she said.

"Did Kevin attempt to use these pictures?" I said.

"No, certainly not."

"Did you know he was dead?" I said.

"No, of course not, how would I? I told you we agreed to be apart."

"You didn't seem to have much reaction when I told you he was dead."

"I know, I... I should. We were very close for a while. But you had just thrust that picture at me.... How did he die?"

"Someone shot him in the back of his head while he was sitting in his car outside a restaurant on Route 9."

"My God."

"Would you have any thoughts on that?" I said.

"How awful."

"Any others?"

"No. You think I... because of the pictures?"

"You said he didn't use the pictures."

"He didn't. I didn't mean that. I just meant you might be suspicious."

I nodded. We were quiet. The snow was still steady, melting as it touched the warm glass walls, turning into glistening rivulets, that distorted the gray light.

"There's a thing that's been bothering me," I said.

She waited.

"Many of these pictures feature you and Kevin together."

She nodded.

"This one is not your standard Polaroid nudie," I said. "Intimate close-ups, longer full shots, interesting perspectives."

She nodded again. There was a deep numbness about her, as if she were slipping further and further below the surface.

"Who took them?" I said.

She stared at me as if she didn't understand the question. I waited. She took in some air and let it out, several times. She opened her mouth and closed it and opened it again.

"What do you mean?" she said.

"Mrs. Patton. You're in a pretty sizable mess," I said. "The only way we are going to get you out of it is if you will talk to me. Who took the pictures?"

She breathed some more and did the mouth-open, mouth-closed thing again. She looked down at the blank back of the photograph, and out the window at the snow, and back at me. She was blushing again.

"Brock," she said.

The name hung in the air between us. She tried to meet my stare but she couldn't hold it, and finally her gaze dropped and then she put her face in her hands.

"Your husband took these pictures of you," I said.

She nodded.

"Did the plumber know?"

"Yes."

"What did he think about it?"

"He was a little embarrassed, but..."

"But?"

"He found me desirable."

"So he didn't care if your husband was standing there with a camera?"

"Well, he still did, a little."

"And?"

"And we..." She cleared her throat. "We gave him money."

Jesus Christ.

Betty sat with her face in her hands. I stood up. There was no reason to stand, it was just that I couldn't bear to do nothing. I walked the length of the room, looking at the snow-fall, and turned around and walked in the other direction, and stopped by the desk.

"Did you reciprocate?" I said.

She didn't move. Every aspect of her was angular and painful.

"What do you mean?"

"Did you take pictures of your husband with other women?"

More silence.

When she finally spoke her voice was thin and hard to hear.

"Yes," she said.

"The Asian women?" I said.

"You... yes. Sometimes."

"What next," I said. "You rent the Fleet Center, invite everybody?"

She didn't speak.

"Here's some things I think," I said. "I think you know that Kevin Humphries was murdered, because I think you agreed to his murder."

Her shoulders hunched tighter.

"Your daughter heard the conversation," I said. "Between you and Cathal Kragan."

Her voice was a thin screech, barely audible.

"Oh God," she said.

"Kragan works for Albert Antonioni, and Antonioni wants your husband to be governor. Humphries threatened to go public with the pictures, and one thing would lead to another and Antonioni's plans would blow right out of the water. He or Kragan got wind of the blackmail, probably from you, and that was the end of Kevin Humphries."

She was crying now, her face still in her hands. It was hard for her to cry; the sobs racked out of her paroxysmally.

"I have that about right, don't I."

She nodded.

"Millicent?" she said.

"She was in the bathroom when you and Kragan agreed to zip Humphries. She heard it. And when Kragan came in to use the bathroom he saw her, looked right at her, and didn't say a word."

"He knew she heard?" Betty Patton said in her strangulated voice.

"He had to have known," I said. "So when he sent a couple of tough guys to get her away from me, you really think he intended to bring her home?"

"He..."

"Do you?"

Again her throat seemed to have closed entirely, and she struggled to swallow. Then she shook her head.

"I don't either."

"My daughter," Betty Patton whispered. "I want my daughter back."

"So she could become the house photographer?" I said.

"You bitch," Betty Patton rasped.

"Yes, you're right. There's no need for that, I'm sorry."

"I don't want them to kill my daughter."

"Good," I said. "We've found common ground."

CHAPTER 52

Billie had brought us some tea, and Betty Patton had poured some brandy into hers, and we had moved to a couple of summery-looking armchairs in the conservatory. The snow was mostly rain now. And the late afternoon had turned dark.

"If you tell me everything you know, maybe I can fix this," I said.

"All of it?"

Betty had made a trip to her room and put herself back together. Her voice was still small, but it no longer sounded as if it were being squeezed from a tube.

"My concern is Millicent," I said. "I will do what seems in her best interest."

"And what of me?"

"I don't know. One salvation at a time," I said.

"That's acceptable," she said.

"Oh good," I said. "Talk."

"I don't... know... where... to begin."

"You said something about, I didn't know what it was like to be married to him. Why don't you tell me?"

"Brock..." She shook her head sadly. "Brock is one of those people for whom too much is never enough. It accounts, I suppose, for his success. He is passionate in pursuit of everything. He always seems to want more. More success, more money, more power, more prominence, more sex, more sex partners, more sexual excitement, more, more, more, more, more, more, more."

"Excelsior," I said.

Betty Patton looked at me blankly for a moment, decided I hadn't said anything worth asking about, and continued.

"At first that excited me. I liked the challenge. I liked..." She made a searching-for-the-right-word motion with her left hand. "I liked the sense of being the one."

"The one who was enough?" I said.

"Yes."

"But you weren't."

"No. It's not like there was someone else." She laughed without amusement. "There was everyone else."

"Equal opportunity," I said, just to be saying something.

"I assume he's made a pass at you," Betty said.

"Yes."

"A lot of women are flattered. He's powerful, rich, handsome."

"I wasn't flattered," I said.

She looked into her tea cup for a minute, holding it in both hands, then drank some, and put the cup on the tabletop.

"He cheated on me from the first day, I guess."

"What did you do?"

"I got even."

"By cheating on him?"

"Yes."

"Did you enjoy that?"

"No."

"Did it bring you closer together?"

"No."

I didn't say anything.

"But it made me feel less like somebody's discarded toy," Betty said. "The worse he got, the worse I became."

"See what you made me do," I said.

She looked at me as if I'd said something puzzling.

"We seemed somehow to fuel each other, we became more perverse and more perverse. I had my plumber. He had his China dolls. I don't remember exactly when we joined forces."

"Joined forces?"

"Yes. I would watch him. He would watch me."

"And the, ah, partners, never minded?" I said.

"At first they didn't know; we had viewing ports."

"Peepholes?"

"Yes."

I was beginning to feel as if I'd spent my life in a convent and was just emerging.

"The strange thing was that it gave us a thing we did together, a, ah, project. We'd plan together who, and how many, and when, and where to meet them, and what to do with them, and that led us to think about photographing them, and then how to do that and we'd buy photography equipment, and, for obvious reasons, we learned how to develop our own pictures. It was the closest we'd been since Millicent was born."

"And no matter what you did, he didn't get jealous."

"No. He seemed to like it."

"Some revenge," I said. "Tell me about Kragan and Antonioni."

"Do you know who they are?" Betty said.

"I know a little," I said. "But go ahead, why don't you tell me whatever you know."

"And this will help Millicent?"

"She will be safe when there's no one walking around with a reason to kill her," I said.

"And you think we can accomplish that?"

"If I know what's going on," I said.

"Is she somewhere safe?"

"Yes," I said, "she's with people who will take care of her."

"Unlike her parents," Betty said.

I waited. Betty poured some more tea for us, and offered me brandy. I shook my head. She put some in her tea and took a sip, and sat back holding the teacup. There was very little light coming in through the wet glass of the conservatory. Had the sun been out it would have been barely visible above the western horizon.

"Brock has long been active in politics," Betty said. "He has been a regular contributor to Republican candidates, and a vigorous fund-raiser as well. And several times he has taken a leave and served in one governmental job or another. Now he is running for governor."

"How do you feel about that?"

"I want it very much. I would like to be First Lady of the Commonwealth, and perhaps it would lead to more."

"And Antonioni was going to help him?"

"He was going to help us. I was very much a part of Brock's campaign."

"Another project," I said.

Again Betty gave me the look that suggested she didn't quite get me. She was not alone. Then she seemed to dismiss the puzzlement and went on talking.

"Albert Antonioni is some sort of mobster from Rhode Island. There is, as you may know, a kind of vacuum in the mob situation here."

"Yes," I said. "And Antonioni wants to fill it."

"Yes. Brock knew Albert when we lived in Rhode Island. We stayed in touch when we moved here. Albert thinks that when he expands into Massachusetts, it would be useful to have a governor he could trust."

"So he has put a lot of money into Brock's campaign."

"Yes."

"And Kragan?"

"Cathal is Albert's man on the scene. Much of what Albert wants to take over is currently owned by the Irish. I think Albert feels the need to have one of their own as a point man. You know how ethnic they all are."

I wasn't sure who *they all* were. But it didn't seem like I needed to at the moment and I let it pass.

"Does Antonioni own your husband?" I said.

Betty drank some of her brandied tea and stared out at the dying light. She nodded slowly.

"Yes," she said.

"So when you made the mistake of giving those pictures to Kevin the plumber, and he made the mistake of trying to blackmail you with them, you went to Antonioni."

"Kragan," she said. "Albert is remote and prefers it that way."

"And that was the conversation your daughter overheard."

"Yes."

"Do you know that she has found some of the pictures you took?"

"She searched my room? She's not ever..."

I didn't say anything. Betty heard herself and stopped.

"She's seen them?"

"Yes."

Betty continued to look out at the dark rain.

"Oh God," she said, "oh my dear God."

CHAPTER 53

Thirty-three King's Beach Terrace was in Swampscott, just over the line from Lynn, facing east across Lynn Shore Drive, where the Atlantic Ocean rolled ashore at King's Beach.

I parked on Lynn Shore Drive. Beside me in the passenger seat, Spike, wearing Oakley wrap-around sunglasses, was drop-dead gorgeous in a blue suit, dark blue shirt, amethyst tie, blue socks with some sort of small, round clock pattern in the weave, and black brogues gleaming with polish. He wore a big showy silk handkerchief in his breast pocket. It matched his tie.

"Spike," I said, "you are better-looking than Leonardo DiCaprio."

"So is Rosie," Spike said. "I just dress better."

"You did bring a gun," I said.

"I don't have one that matches," Spike said.

"But you brought one."

Spike grinned and opened his coat so I could see the butt of his Army Colt.

"I know you've explained it before," Spike said, "but this Cathal Kragan is a stone killer, right?"

"Yes."

"And why is it just you and me are calling on him?"

"I'm going to have to ask Richie for help if I need to talk with Albert Antonioni. I wasn't comfortable asking him for help with Kragan."

"He wouldn't have even had to come," Spike said. "His uncle could have come out with six or eight pistoleros and Kragan would have stood at attention while you talked with him."

"Not the best way for me to learn anything," I said. "And even if it were, I can't ask him."

"How about the cop you're bopping?"

I shook my head.

"Something?" Spike said.

"I'm afraid he's getting too serious."

"So exploit that," Spike said.

"No," I said.

"Jesus Christ," Spike said. "I gotta be pals with Nancy fucking Drew."

"Are you scared?"

"I am without fear," Spike said. "As you know. But if I were going to acquire some, this would be a good place to start."

I opened the car door and got out.

"Don't worry about it," I said. "You're with me, after all."

Spike climbed out of his side of the car and shut the door.

"True," he said. "And I look so goddamned good."

Kragan's front door was opened by a bright-faced woman in her forties with a mass of dark red hair. A reddish dachshund peeked between her feet growling and wagging its tail. Talk about mixed messages. The woman held the dog back with one foot.

"My name is Sunny Randall," I said. "I called earlier. Could you tell Mr. Kragan I'm here?"

"Sure, I'll tell him," the woman said. "Excuse me, but I have to close the door so the dog won't get out."

"I understand," I said.

Spike and I stood and looked at the ocean for a little while and the door opened again. The red-haired woman stepped aside and we went into the foyer. The dog was no longer in evidence.

"Right over here," the woman said, "in the living room."

He was just as Millicent had described him: squat, thick-bodied, silver-haired, impeccable, and alive with force. He was sitting in an armchair by a fireplace with a gas fire, looking a bit posed, and incredibly, wearing a green velvet smoking jacket. Standing by the archway that led to the living room was a guy that looked like the employee of the month for Bodyguards-R-Us. He was about two hundred and fifty pounds of bone and muscle, padded by at least a hundred pounds of fat. He glanced at Spike with amusement.

Kragan spoke in the deep purr that I'd heard on my answering machine.

"So you're Sunny Randall," he said.

"Yes."

"Who's the clotheshorse?"

"My friend Spike," I said.

"What's he doing here?"

"Design police," Spike said. "Gas fireplaces are really tacky."

Kragan's expression never changed.

"Georgie," he said, "get him out of here."

Georgie said, "Out you go, Mary."

He put his hand on Spike's chest and shoved him toward the hallway. Spike hit him four or five karate-type chops, too fast for an accurate count, and Georgie fell down and lay gasping on the floor. While he was going down I took my gun out in case Kragan took offense. If he did, he didn't show it. He seemed mildly interested in how quick Spike was. Spike leaned over and patted Georgie down and took a gun away from him. He removed the magazine and put it in his pocket. He racked the slide back and ejected the shell from the chamber, and dropped the gun back onto the floor beside Georgie.

"He gonna recover?" Kragan said.

"Few minutes," Spike said. "I didn't go full out."

Kragan nodded. "Be sort of interesting sometime to see you go full out," he said.

"I didn't come here to cause trouble," I said.

"You brought him for that?" Kragan said.

"I brought him to protect me," I said.

"So far he's doing a hell of a job of it," Kragan said, "You don't need the piece."

I put my gun away. Kragan appeared to pay no further attention to Georgie. Spike leaned against the wall near the door, rubbing his hands gently.

"There's a Boston cop named Kelly," I said. "And a couple of members of the Desmond Burke family that know I'm here."

I was lying, but Kragan didn't know that.

"Being pretty careful," he said.

"I don't want you to make any mistakes," I said. "You made one already and Georgie paid for it."

Kragan waved his left hand dismissively.

"So what do you want?" he said.

"You're trying to kill Millicent Patton," I said.

"Really?"

"Un huh. And me, too, while you're at it."

"You, too?" Kragan said.

"She heard you and her mother talk about killing a man who turned out to be a plumber from Framingham named Kevin Humphries."

"She tell you that?" Kragan said.

Georgie had slowly gotten his breathing under control and was now sitting up on the floor, trying to get oriented.

"You killed him because Albert Antonioni told you to," I said.

"Who's Albert Antonioni?"

"Antonioni wants to move into Massachusetts and to have his own governor in office when he does. The plumber had pictures of himself and Betty Patton that would ruin the governor plans."

"So?"

"So he had you kill the plumber. But the girl heard you and her mother planning it, so the girl had to go, too. Otherwise the whole story comes out and puts you and Albert inside, not outside," I said.

"And you can prove all of this?" Kragan said.

"I can prove enough of this to give you a lot of grief."

"Say the girl did hear me, which she didn't, but say for the moment I believe your fairy tale. All she heard was an agreement to kill somebody. How do you tie that to the plumber?"

I almost bit. My mouth had actually opened before I closed it. If he knew that I thought I could turn Betty Patton, then he would kill her. I waited a moment before I spoke and breathed in a couple of times through my nose and thought a couple of sentences ahead. Then I answered.

"I can't," I said.

"So?"

"I'm not after you," I said. "I'm after Albert Antonioni."

"And?"

"Somebody's going to have to go down on this thing. I thought maybe we could work a trade—him for you."

As he leaned against the wall, Spike was absently thumbing the shells from the magazine he'd taken from Georgie's gun. Georgie had gotten unsteadily to his feet and gone to the couch, where he sat now, not feeling very well.

"And all you got is the kid's story," Kragan said.

"That's all I've got, yet."

Kragan laughed.

"Come back when you got more," he said.

"Such as who popped Bucko Meehan," I said.

"Well, you are a nosy little girl, aren't you."

Spike finished emptying the magazine and put the shells into his coat pocket.

"Yes," I said, "I am, and stubborn and annoying. But a lovely person for all of that."

"You're like a housefly," Kragan said slowly,

his voice so deep that some of it seemed to drop out as he talked. "Don't do no real damage. But you keep buzzing around until you irritate somebody, and then you get swatted."

"This is your last chance," I said. "Do you want to be the one who gets the break or not?"

Kragan didn't speak, but he made a gesture with his hand as if he were swatting a fly, and he looked at me straight on as he did it, and I felt a little thrill of fear dart through my stomach.

"Well," I said. "You better send somebody better than Georgie."

Kragan kept looking at me.

"It won't be Georgie," he said.

I looked at Spike. He shrugged. I nodded and started out of the living room. Spike tossed the empty magazine on the floor beside the gun.

"Nobody's wearing smoking jackets anymore," he said to Kragan, and followed me out.

CHAPTER 54

"I know Georgie McPhail," Richie said. "He used to do strong-arm collection for a loan shark named Murray Vee."

"What kind of name is Vee?" I said.

"Short for a long funny name, I never knew what it was."

We were sitting at Spike's kitchen table. Richie and Millicent had just come back from the movies. Spike was cooking venison sausage with vinegar peppers on his big six-burner professional-looking stove. Rosie had located the sausages with her keen nose and was now immobilized on the floor under Spike's feet, pointing them.

"Georgie isn't that easy to take."

"Like Grant took Richmond," Spike said and shook the long-handled sauté pan briskly.

"Could you win a fight with him?" Millicent asked.

Richie smiled at her.

"Don't know," he said. "I never tried."

"Richie could take Georgie McPhail," Spike said from the stove. "He's pretty tough for a straight guy."

Richie grinned.

"Did the Kragan man say anything about me?" Millicent said.

"No," I said. "I did most of the talking."

"What did you talk about?"

"I offered him a chance to cooperate with us in our investigation," I said.

"And Spike really beat up a guy?"

"He was protecting me," I said.

"What did the Kragan man say?"

"He said he didn't want to cooperate."

"So you went through all that for nothing?" Millicent said.

"Well, maybe not for nothing," I said. "It might get something to happen."

"What?"

"I don't know, but anything is better than nothing. Things happen, I can react to them. Nothing happens, I have nothing to do."

"But what if the something that happens is bad?"

"I expect to deal with it," I said. "It's better than nothing happening."

Millicent shook her head.

"My parents better be paying you a ton of money for this," she said.

I didn't say anything. Spike cut a small bite of sausage, checked to see if it was done, blew on it to cool it, and then scraped it off the fork and let it drop into Rosie's quick jaws.

"They're not paying her anything," Spike said. "They fired her a long time ago."

"Fired her?"

"Yeah. When she wouldn't give you back to them."

Millicent stared at Spike for a long time. But she didn't say anything. Then she shifted her gaze to Rosie. She didn't look at me.

"Can you get me to Albert Antonioni?" I said to Richie.

"Yes. But it'll probably have to include my father and my uncle."

"Okay," I said. "As soon as you can."

"It'll include me, too," Richie said.

"That's good," I said.

"I'd have backed you up with Kragan if you'd asked," Richie said quietly.

"I know. I couldn't ask."

"But you could ask Spike."

276

"Spike is not my ex-husband," I said.

"But you can ask me to set you up with Antonioni."

"I don't fully understand it, Richie. I am feeling my way along—with this case, with you, with her—I wish I knew what I was doing, but I don't. So I have to go by what feels right, and it didn't feel right to ask you to back me up with Kragan."

"But it feels okay to use my family's influence to get you to Antonioni."

"Actually," I said, "it doesn't. But I have nowhere else to go, and I need to do this, so..." I shrugged and turned my palms up.

Spike was discreetly busy with the sausage and peppers. But Millicent was young enough to feel no need for discretion. She was leaning forward, fascinated with the exchange.

"I'll set it up," Richie said.

Spike put the peppers onto a cold burner, and added two big handfuls of pasta to a large pot that was already boiling.

I said to Millicent, "Do you think your mother loves you?"

"What?"

I said it again.

"I don't..."

Her shoulders stiffened and her body got that pained angular look I'd come to recognize.

"No. I don't think so," she said.

"If you found that she did, could you love her back?"

"I hate her," Millicent said.

Her voice was flat, and she seemed once again

the sullen little girl I had dragged away from a pimp.

"But if she changed," I said. "And it was clear that she loved you and was different than she had been, could you love her?"

"You trying to get rid of me?"

"Millicent," I said. "If I haven't proved that I care about you by now, I'm not going to be able to prove it."

"Then why are you asking?"

"Because I want to know. If you and your mother could be together and help each other to be happy, it would be a good thing."

"But I don't have to."

"You can stay with me as long as you need to," I said.

I felt a twinge of dismay in the bottom of my stomach. I did not want a teenaged daughter. I felt like I still was one.

"You're nice to me," Millicent said in a very small voice.

"Yes," I said. "You deserve to be treated well. I am beginning to think that your mother might love you. That she might be capable of change. We won't hurry that. But I just want you to keep an open mind. Remember no one will force you to do anything."

Millicent nodded. Her posture eased a little. Spike placed a large basket of French bread on the table. Then he took the pot off the stove and poured the pasta into a colander in the sink and let it drain and dumped it onto a platter. He distributed the sausage and peppers over it and plonked the platter in the center of the table.

"Red wine?" he said.

"Be fools not to," Richie said.

Spike began to unscrew a big jug of Cabernet. Rosie, tracking the sausage, trotted over and jumped up into Richie's lap where she was eye level with her quarry.

"Richie," I said, "I don't think she should be at the table."

"Don't be so bossy," Richie said.

"That's right," Spike said.

"You are kind of bossy," Millicent said.

I looked around at the odd gathering. Then I broke off a small piece of French bread and gave it to Rosie.

"Oh, bite my clank," I said.

CHAPTER 55

I bought some new place settings to make up for the ones that had been vandalized, and I took them to the empty loft and carefully set my table with them and stood back and looked at them.

"Very nice," I said.

On my bed, Rosie raised her head and looked at me.

"You like?" I said.

She stared at me and kept her opinion to herself.

I fussed with the table setting for a while and

then put Rosie's leash on and went down to my car. It was early evening, still sort of half lit with a blue tone, as I put the car in gear and drove away from my loft. As I always did these days, I circled the block once to see if I could spot anyone following me. I didn't see anyone, but, as I came back to Summer Street, a black Lexus settled in behind me. It didn't have to be a tail. This was a prime route out of South Boston. Past South Station I took a left and headed past Chinatown toward the expressway. There was a lot of traffic. The car behind me did the same thing. In fact ten cars behind me did the same thing. Most of them peeled off toward the Southeast Expressway, but at least three of us deked and dived among the pylons and construction hazards and onto the Mass Pike heading west. The Lexus cruised past me. It had tinted windows and I couldn't see the driver. Maybe I was jumpy because of the vandalism in my loft, and the way Kragan had looked at me when Spike and I left him. On the other hand, there was no exit until we got to Allston so he could tail me from in front without worrying that I'd turn off on him. We went under the Pruden-tial Center and past Fenway Park and behind B.U. The sign said Cambridge/Allston; as I pulled into the right lane to exit, I passed the black Lexus and when I went off, he was behind me. At the river, I turned right onto Storrow Drive. If he was tailing me he'd have to show himself. There wasn't much reason for someone to come out here on the Pike and then head right back into town. As I passed B.U. from this side, he was behind me. I felt the little thrill of fear again. I looked at Rosie. She was on the floor of the passenger side with her nose almost in the heater. Good. She was out of the line of fire. I took my gun out and put it in my lap.

At the overpass to the Fens the Lexus began to close on me. I took the Fenway exit and cut over to Mass Avenue and went south. The Lexus was right behind me now, and as we approached Washington Street the Lexus pulled out as if to pass me. A window in the back seat rolled down. I slammed on my brakes as hard as I could and a shotgun blast went sweeping over the hood of my car. I yanked the car left onto Washington Street. Behind me I could hear the tires squealing on the Lexus. I was heading for the police station on Warren Ave., but I wasn't going to make it. There was a red light two blocks ahead. Cars were stopped in both directions. If I got stuck in traffic I was dead. But I had a backup. I yanked the car right, and then right again onto Tremont and jammed it up on the sidewalk in front of Buddy's Fox. Tony Marcus. It wasn't much but there wasn't anything else. I picked up my gun, scooped Rosie up and ran in the front door. The place was full. Everyone was black, and most of them were male. I went to the bar.

"Tony Marcus," I said. "My name's Sunny Randall."

I could tell that the bartender had seen the gun. But all he said was, "Hold on."

He must have hit a button under the bar

because all of a sudden Junior appeared in the hallway with Ty-Bop jittering beside him. Kragan came into the restaurant with two other men. All three had their hands in their pockets. Tony Marcus slid past Junior and stood beside me at the bar.

"Sunny Randall," he said, and reached out and scratched Rosie behind the ear.

Kragan glanced around the restaurant and then began to walk toward me.

"He wants to kill me," I said to Tony.

"We don't want him doing none of that," Marcus said and stepped in front of me. "Do we?"

"Step away from her," Kragan said.

Tony looked at Ty-Bop, and a gun appeared in Ty-Bop's hand as if it had always been there.

"He show a piece," Tony jerked his head at Kragan, "kill him."

From his post in the hallway Junior produced a double-barreled shotgun. The bartender showed a pump gun. Both shotguns were aimed at Kragan's companions. Kragan looked at Ty-Bop. Ty-Bop looked back at him without expression. He was suddenly motionless, as if the gun had stabilized him. His small eyes had the depth and humanity of two bottle caps. It was as if his life was in his gun. Kragan looked at him the way a huge crocodile might suddenly confront a small, very poisonous viper. In Kragan's face was the slowly dawning realization that this trivial boy could kill him. Him! Cathal Kragan! The restaurant was dead silent. The diners all hunched a little lower over their tables, trying to watch, trying not to get caught watching, hoping that if the guns went off they wouldn't get hit.

"You motherfuckers have a reservation?" Tony said.

Nobody said anything. Kragan couldn't seem to take his eyes off me. His desire to kill me seemed almost sensual.

"No?" Tony said, just as if Kragan had answered. "Then get the fuck out of my restaurant."

Nothing moved.

"I say three, and you ain't moving," Tony Marcus said to Kragan. "Then Ty-Bop going to shoot you in the head. One..."

Kragan moved. Without a word he turned and walked out. The two backup men went out after him. The room was quiet for a moment, then someone began to clap and then somebody else clapped, and then everyone in the restaurant began to applaud.

"Join us for supper, Sunny," Tony Marcus said. "Later on I'll have somebody take you home."

"I couldn't eat," I said.

"How 'bout this animal here, she like chitlins?"

"I don't think so," I said.

"Never liked them much either," Tony said.

56

I was in a big round booth at the back of a coffee shop opposite the green in Taunton with three Burkes and two Antonionis. I was the only female.

"I had heard that your son was divorced from this lady, Desmond." Albert Antonioni said.

"What's between them is not our business," Richie's father said. "Richie says she's still family."

He was thin Irish—hollow cheeks, deep-set eyes. He had the look of Irish martyrdom about him, like some pale priest willing to starve to death for Ireland's freedom. His brother Felix, Richie's uncle, had once been a heavy-weight boxer, and he bore the marks of it. There were scars around his eyes. His nose was thick and flat. His neck was short and his upper body was thick and slightly round-shouldered, as if the weight of all that muscle had begun to tire him.

"We have no problem with you," Antonioni said.

He had a white beard and a strong nose, and his dark eyes moved very quickly. His son Allie was beside him, bigger than his father and clean-shaven, but with the same nose, and the same quick eyes.

"You do, if you have a problem with Sunny," Desmond said.

At the next table were men who had come with the Antonionis. That made four on their side, and four on ours, including me. I was flattered. I knew that these things were worked out as meticulously as the seating at the Paris peace conference, and I had been counted as a full person.

Before we'd come Richie had said to me, "Don't get feminist on me in this one. These guys live in a male world. We'll get what we want better if you are, ah, ladylike."

"Can I say fuck now and then," I had asked, "just to be one of the guys?"

Richie smiled.

"You will never be one of the guys," he said. "The less you say, the better it'll go."

I knew he was right, and now, on scrupulously neutral territory—about halfway between Providence and Boston, a little closer to Providence, to show Antonioni some respect, but still in Massachusetts, to show the Burkes respect—I was sitting beside Richie, letting Desmond Burke do the talking. Richie was as quiet as I was.

"I don't think we have a problem with Sunny that can't be worked out," Antonioni said. "We got some plans. We been careful making those plans, we don't interfere with your plans."

"I got no problem with your plans, Albert. There's too many lone cowhands in Boston since Gerry went down. Fast Eddie got Chinatown, Tony got the niggers, we got ours. You come in and organize the rest, it'll save me doing it. I don't want to do it. I'm happy with what I got."

"I appreciate that," Antonioni said.

"But you can't be fucking with any of us, excuse me, Sunny."

I smiled modestly.

"Didn't know we were, Desmond."

"Now you do," Felix said.

Felix had taken a couple too many punches in the neck. His voice sounded the way I'd always imagined a rhinoceros might sound clearing its throat. Antonioni smiled faintly.

"We ain't afraid of you," he said.

Neither Desmond nor Felix said anything.

"On the other hand we don't need no fucking two-front war," Antonioni said. "Begging your pardon, Sunny."

I smiled modestly. No one else said anything.

"So whaddya need," Antonioni said.

Desmond nodded at me.

"I need the Patton girl safe," I said.

"She's witness to a murder conspiracy," Antonioni said.

"I need someone for the murder, too," I said.

Antonioni sat back in his seat and looked at me.

"Who'd you have in mind," Antonioni said.

"Kragan tried to kill the girl and me. I assume he did the plumber."

Antonioni looked at his son. His son nodded.

"Cathal zipped him," the son said.

"And Bucko Meehan."

"He did that on his own," Allie said.

"You want Cathal?" Antonioni said.

"Yes."

"You know why Cathal zipped the plumber?" Antonioni said.

"Pictures," I said.

Antonioni nodded slowly.

"You know our interest in that?"

"Governor," I said.

Antonioni smiled again. It was an odd smile, nearly invisible. But it was real. It was the smile of a man who had once been able to laugh.

"I like a quiet woman," he said.

He drank some coffee.

"Cold," he said, and handed his cup to one of the men at the next table. The man got up and went for fresh coffee. "How you going to take Cathal down without messing up what I got in place with Patton?"

"Maybe I can't," I said.

Antonioni's new coffee arrived. He sipped some and nodded once.

"Better," he said.

He put the cup down and looked straight at me.

"We got a problem," he said.

"We didn't have a problem," Desmond Burke said, "we wouldn't be sitting here trying to solve it."

Antonioni nodded. Everyone was quiet. Desmond looked at me.

"Whaddya want to do, Sunny?" he said.

"I want the girl safe," I said.

Desmond looked at Antonioni.

"I can give you that," Albert said. "But I can't

guarantee Kragan. Kid could bury him if she testified."

"I can put Kragan in jail," I said.

"But will he go quiet?" Albert said.

"You tell me," I said. "What about omertà and all that."

"Kragan's Irish," Allie said. "They don't have no vow of silence."

"Even if he was straight from Palermo," Albert said, "things are different than they was. Omertà don't look so good, you're facing fucking three hundred years hard time."

"Maybe I could leave Brock Patton alone," I said.

Again everyone was quiet. Albert blew on his coffee a little, then sipped some. He looked at Allie. They looked at each other for a moment.

"Maybe we could straighten things out with Kragan," Albert said.

"That would work," I said.

On the ride home, alone together in my car, Richie said to me, "They're going to kill him, you know."

"Kragan?"

"Yep."

"I sort of figured they would," I said.

Richie was quiet. I could feel him looking at me as I drove.

"You're a pretty tough cookie," he said.

"Thank you for noticing."

CHAPTER 57

Allie Antonioni had called Felix and told him
that Albert wanted him to tell Desmond that
Kragan was decommissioned. Desmond told
Richie and Richie had told me. I could go home.
The long exile was over. I was back in my loft.
Rosie was sleeping on my bed, nearly invisible among the pillows. Millicent was with
Richie; and I was entertaining her mother at
my kitchen table. We talked for nearly four
hours. Occasionally she cried. When she did
I waited. When she stopped, we talked some
more. By the time her husband arrived I was
quite tired. But we had a plan.

"Tea?" I said. "Coffee?"

"I have no time for this," Brock Patton
said to me. "I'm not running some kind of ma
and pa store. What the hell am I here for?"

I poured some more tea for Betty Patton and
for me and gestured with the teapot at Brock.
He shook his head.

"For God's sake get on with it," he said.

He was vibrantly impatient with female
silliness.

"I think I can keep most of this secret," I
said.

"Excuse me?"

"The womanizing, the Asian girls." I said.
"The gang bangs. The picture taking, the
voyeurism. Of course I don't have to keep it

secret. If you annoy me, I can get even by blab-
bing to everyone."

"You have no evidence."

"I have talked with your wife and she's
prepared to go public, if she needs to."

"That would be a very dangerous thing for
anyone to do," Patton said.

"No, it won't be. I have talked with your
owner, Albert Antonioni. He will follow my
lead."

"I don't believe you."

I shrugged.

"My wife won't speak a word," Patton said.

I looked at Betty Patton.

"Yes," she said. "I will."

"A wife can't testify against her husband."

"Depends," I said. "But in any case she
can talk to the press."

"She'd be publicly humiliated."

"I'm humiliated now," Betty Patton said.
"By what I've become. By what I've allowed
you to turn me into."

"Oh, you didn't want to make it with every
plumber and delivery man that came to the
door. You didn't want me to become governor
and maybe someday president, you weren't
pushing me, pushing me, like Lady Macbeth.
Big bad old me *made* you do all that."

"I started out wanting you to love me,"
she said.

"That was a while ago," he said.

"Yes, it was," she said. "And then I wanted
at least to be able to love you. And then I wanted

at least to get even, and then I wanted to get what I thought you owed me, even if we had no marriage."

"And now what, you want to destroy me?"

"I want to save my daughter."

"Oh God, motherhood," Brock said. "Isn't it a little late for motherly self-sacrifice?"

"If I can save her, maybe I can save myself," Betty said.

Brock looked at me.

"Women!" he said. "Do you have any thoughts on how to clean up this mess?"

"I do," I said. "Thank you for asking."

I gave him my most charming smile. Some men sink to their knees when I give my most ingratiating smile. Patton bore up under it manfully.

"You and Albert can stay in business," I said. "And Betty will not say anything about you to anyone. Cathal Kragan takes the fall for Kevin Humphries's murder."

"Who's Kevin Humphries?" Patton said.

"Plumber from Framingham." I said. "Was passing out pictures."

"And when Kragan, as you so thoughtfully put it, takes the fall," Patton said. "What ensures his silence?"

"I have Antonioni's assurance that Kragan will be quiet," I said.

Patton looked at his wife. She didn't speak, but her head was up and she looked at him steadily.

"And what is required of me?" he said.

"You set up an irrevocable trust fund for your wife and daughter. With my humble self as trustee. Amount of the fund to come."

"So you can embezzle from me?"

"Once the fund was in place, I'd actually be embezzling from Millicent," I said. "The fund will be large enough to cover the cost of psychotherapy for Millicent and for her mother."

Patton stood and rested his hands flat on the tabletop and glowered down at his wife and me.

"Do you... have... any idea... who you're... dealing with?"

I nodded.

"I can have you killed, for Christ sake."

I shook my head.

"Oh?" Patton said. "You don't think so?"

"Albert Antonioni suggested you call him when we got to this point."

"Are you kidding?"

I reached behind me, picked up the phone on the kitchen counter, and dialed.

"Mr. Antonioni please," I said. "Sunny Randall."

I waited. In a moment Allie came on the line.

"This is Allie."

"I have Brock Patton here," I said. "One moment."

Patton's face was gray. But he took the phone.

"This is Brock Patton," he said.

He listened for a moment.

"You know this broad, Allie?"

292

He listened again. For several moments, nodding his head slightly.

"Right," he said. "Right."

He listened again.

"Sure, Allie," he said. "Absolutely."

Then he hung up. His face still looked gray, and his eyes seemed very tired.

"Okay," he said. "That's the deal. Have your attorney send me the trust agreement."

He looked at Betty Patton.

"What about you?" he said.

"I'm not coming home," she said.

"Fine," he said. "There's a hundred others just like you."

"I know," she said.

He looked at me.

"You're a smart little bitch," he said, "aren't you."

"I'm not so little," I said.

He turned and stalked out of my loft and slammed the door, which roused Rosie. She sat up among the pillows looking annoyed. Rosie jumped down from the bed and came briskly the length of the loft and jumped up in my lap and began to lap my neck. Betty Patton folded her arms on the tabletop and put her head down.

"Oh God," she said.

"You did good," I said.

"I still have to face Millicent."

"I know."

"I don't know what to say."

"Tell her the truth," I said. "Tell her what you did and why you did it and how you are going to try and change and why. Don't talk down to her. Don't give her orders."

"I've forfeited any rights I had to order her around," Betty said. "Brock is right, it is crazy now to try to be a mother."

"Don't aim so high right away," I said. "Maybe you can learn to be friends in a while. And then maybe you can be an older friend, one who is helpful, one who can offer guidance, one who can love her, one who seems to be sort of like a mother."

Betty raised her head.

"Do you have a wonderful mother, Sunny?"

"Not especially," I said.

"Then how do you know all this?"

"Remember," I said, "I'm a smart little bitch."

CHAPTER 58

I had never been able to do the same painting over again, so, since my Chinatown had been destroyed, I was working on a view of the old Charles Street jail. Rosie was lying on the rug near me, and Millicent was reading the paper in bed. We had agreed on no television when I was trying to work. It was a rule for me. I couldn't stand television and when I'm working I need to be able to focus. But there was a happy and entirely accidental by-product of the rule. She had started to read the paper.... Could a book be far behind?

I was busy trying to get the right gray for the jail when Rosie sat up suddenly and looked at the door. I picked up my gun from the table next to me. The doorbell rang. Rosie dashed to the door barking and being fearsome, but her tail was wagging furiously, which meant it was probably Richie. I checked through the peephole. It wasn't Richie. It was Brian. I opened the door. Brian came in and closed the door behind him and leaned forward and kissed me lightly.

"I figured I better do that," he said, "or you might shoot."

I smiled and put the gun on the table. Brian waved at Millicent.

"I might have," I said. "Would you like coffee?"

"Sure."

Brian went and looked at my painting while I measured out the coffee and water.

"You decided not to paint Chinatown?" he said.

"I can't do the same painting again," I said. "Maybe later."

"Why is that?"

"I have no idea."

"Artistic temperament?"

"I suspect that *artistic temperament* is bullshit," I said. "Rembrandt and van Gogh were both artists, but I doubt that they had similar temperaments."

We sat at my counter. I poured coffee. We

both added milk. I used Equal in mine, Brian put sugar in his. Rosie sat at his feet, ever hopeful.

"No donuts?" he said.

"I didn't know there was going to be a cop in the house," I said.

We were quiet for a moment.

"Cathal Kragan turned up in Chelsea Creek this morning," Brian said.

"Dead?"

Brian nodded.

"Shot behind his right ear," he said. "At an up angle. Bullet exited in front above his left eye."

"Good," I said.

"You have any idea how that came to pass?" Brian said.

"Yes."

"But you don't want to share?"

"It's not something you should know," I said.

"Not you?" Brian said.

"No."

"You have anything to do with it?"

"I might have gotten the ball rolling," I said.

"Richie Burke?"

"No."

Brian paused for a moment and thought.

"Richie put you in touch," he said. "His family applied some pressure."

"Maybe," I said. "Are you sorry he's dead?"

"Hell, no," Brian said. "I'm just trying to figure out where to send the medal. You want me to call Framingham, let them know?"

"No," I said. "I'll call Anderson. He was a pretty good guy in all of this."

"Me, too," Brian said.

"Yes," I said. "Especially you, too."

Again we were quiet. Brian reached over and poured himself more coffee.

"So it's over," he said.

"Except for Millicent," I said.

"How about us," Brian said. "Is it over for us?"

I felt myself tense. I knew we'd have to have this conversation, but I didn't like it any better because I knew it was coming. I nodded slowly.

"Yes," I said.

Brian's face was tight, and his eyes were flat. He wasn't liking this conversation either.

"Richie?" he said.

"Yes."

Brian scratched Rosie's chin with his toe. I'm sure he wasn't aware that he did it.

"You together again?"

"No."

"Then... ?"

"We're not apart enough either," I said.

"Don't you think maybe you ought to come to some terms with that?" Brian said.

"Yes."

"But you haven't."

"Not yet," I said.

"He was very helpful to you through this bad patch with Kragan and all," Brian said.

"Yes."

"Don't be fooled by gratitude," Brian said.

I nodded.

"I hope I'm not."

Brian drank some coffee. The lines at the corners of his mouth had deepened.

"Well, people don't love you just because you want them to," he said.

"I know."

"We did have fun," he said.

"Yes," I said. "We did, and if it stayed fun, it could have gone on. I can have fun without Richie. But it was becoming more than fun. And I'm not sure I can have more than fun with anyone but Richie."

"Well," Brian said, "if you find that you can, check with me, see if I'm free."

"You're a very lovely man, Brian. You deserve more than I have available right now."

"I'd settle for what you have," he said.

"I know," I said. "That's the sad part. But we both know it wouldn't work out. Once you had it you'd want more, and you'd have a right to more, and there wouldn't be more, and... it would be bad."

Brian stood.

"You're right," he said. "I wish you weren't, but I'm too old to pretend you're not."

I stood with him. And put my arms around his waist. He kissed me. And we stood in that embrace for a while.

"I hope you and Richie work it out," he said. "Either way. I hope you settle it."

His voice was hoarse. I nodded. I was too close to crying to say anything. He stepped away from me and went to the door and opened it.

"See you around, Sunny Randall," he said.

And the door closed behind him. Rosie sniffed vigorously at it, her tail wagging fast, as Brian went down the stairs.

CHAPTER 59

I sat back down at the counter in my kitchen and looked at the empty coffee cups for a time. Millicent got off the bed, left the newspaper in a disorganized pile, and came and sat down at the counter beside me. Neither of us said anything for a bit. Rosie joined us, looking up from the floor, and thumping her tail.

"Cathal Kragan is dead," I said.

"Brian told you that?"

"Yes."

"Who killed him?"

"Albert Antonioni," I said.

"Good."

We sat quietly some more. The loft was quiet.

Finally Millicent said, "You broke up with him."

"Yes," I said. "Could you hear?"

"Some," Millicent said.

"I hope it didn't embarrass you," I said.

"No," Millicent said. "I'm glad I heard."

"Because?" I said.

"Because it was so nice. You didn't yell at

each other. You were both nice to each other even if it wasn't working out."

"You understand why it wasn't working out?"

"You're still in love with Richie."

I wanted to say no, it's more complicated than that, but maybe it wasn't. Maybe that's all there was to it. Which was a lot.

"I guess," I said.

"It'll work out," she said.

"Wait a minute," I said, "who's looking out for whom?"

"Whom?"

"Yes," I said. "Whom."

We both smiled a little.

"What about me?" Millicent said.

"What about you?"

"Well, you got rid of Brian," she said. "And that man Cathal is dead. What are you going to say to my father and mother about me?"

"Your father has agreed to fund a trust for your support and education with me as trustee," I said.

"Explain that to me," she said.

"I decide how much money you can have and for what. He has no say about it."

"He wouldn't do that. Why did he say he would?"

"Because your mother and I can ruin him if he doesn't," I said.

"Would you?"

"You bet."

"Would she?"

"Yes."

"You want me to go back and live with them?"

"No," I said. "There's no *them,* anyway. Your mother has left your father."

"Really?"

I nodded.

"Good," Millicent said. "Can I stay with you?"

"Yes," I said. "But here's how I'd like to see it work. My friend Julie will get you an appointment with a good psychiatrist, and you'll see him or her for as long as we all think you should."

"Who's 'we'?"

"Me, you, and the shrink," I said.

"You think there's something wrong with me?"

"You can't have lived the life you've led without needing to fix some things," I said.

"Like what?"

"That's for you and the shrink to decide," I said.

"Maybe you and Richie ought to go," Millicent said, and the shadow of a smile passed across her small face.

"Probably," I said.

"What about my mom and dad?"

"Your father's job is to fund the trust. He does that, we have no need to see him further, unless you want to."

Millicent shook her head.

"Your mother will also see a shrink," I said.

"Same one?"

"No."

"I gotta see her?"

"No."

"Good."

"But remember that, in the end, horrible as she has been, when she understood that she was putting your life in danger, she came down out of the trees."

Millicent nodded. There was no warmth in the nod.

"I don't like her," Millicent said.

"I don't blame you. What I'd like, though, if you could, would be that you'd agree to let her visit you maybe once in a while for an hour."

"No."

"With me present," I said.

Millicent shook her head.

"Okay. Maybe later you'll change your mind." I smiled. "It's supposed to be our prerogative."

"Who?"

"Women," I said.

"Like us," Millicent said.

"Yes."

She sat for a long time staring at the countertop.

"I guess I'll do it if you think I should," she said.

"I do," I said. "But sooner or later you're going to have to decide things because you think you should."

"How can I do that," Millicent said. She raised her head and stared straight at me. Her eyes were glistening with tears. "I don't know anything."

"You know one of the hard things about being a woman," I said, "is having some built-in compass that doesn't depend on others."

"I don't know what you mean," Millicent said.

"When you're talking to a male," I said. "And you want to urge him to do the right thing you can say, 'Be a man.' "

Millicent nodded. Her eyes still shiny. No tears ran. But they didn't go away either.

"That implies some rules of behavior that come from inside," I said. "But if I tell you that maybe your goal is to be a woman, that implies what? Being compassionate? Being a good caregiver? Being sexually attractive? Cooking well?"

I was surprised at what I was saying, and how strongly I was saying it. I felt like Simone de Beauvoir.

"Being a woman implies being in a male context," I said. "Being a man implies being fully yourself. You understand what I'm saying?"

"I don't know," Millicent said. The tears that had filled her eyes were running down her face now. She bent over and picked Rosie up and held her in her lap and hugged her. Rosie lapped Millicent's face. Yum. Salt.

"I guess," Millicent said with her voice shaking, "I just want to be like you, Sunny."

For a moment I thought I might cry, too.

"Excellent choice," I said.

I leaned forward and put my arms around her. It gave Rosie a chance to lap both our faces. Which she did.

60

We were naked and profoundly contumescent. In the darkness, in Richie's bed, we lay together with his arm around my shoulder and my head against his chest.

"A long time coming," Richie said.

"Nice choice of words," I said.

"You know what I mean."

"Yes," I said.

"Where do we go from here?"

"I wish I knew."

"I know some things we don't want to do," Richie said.

"Like?"

"Like rush out and get married."

"No," I said. "We don't want to do that."

"Doesn't mean we won't do it again someday."

"Well," I said. "We did it once."

I couldn't see his face in the darkness, but I could feel Richie smile.

"What would you like?" Richie said.

I was quiet. I felt the way Millicent must have. What in God's name did I want?

"I want to live the way I do," I said.

"Alone?"

"Alone, paint, be a detective, take care of Rosie, get my degree."

"Okay," Richie said.

"I don't need your permission," I said.

Again in the dark I could feel him smile.

"No," he said. "You don't."

"I can't imagine a life for me," I said, "that doesn't have you in it."

"Good."

I remembered it all as I lay there. How his skin smelled, how the hair on his chest felt, how his beard scraped a little even if he had just shaved. I felt the stillness in him.

"I can't imagine," I said again.

"I could be your boyfriend," Richie said.

"Exclusive?" I said.

"Why don't we let each of us decide how we want to be," Richie said.

Jesus Christ. He had never said anything like that before. I was very careful.

"You mean I could date somebody else?" I said.

"Yes," he said. "I could, too."

I felt the shimmer of jealousy tingle through my chest.

"I don't know if that will work," I said.

"If it doesn't we'll modify it," Richie said. "Be good to start this time with no rules."

"You were the one with the rules last time," I said.

"Now I'm not," Richie said.

Richie's place was on the waterfront. In the stillness I could hear the movement of the ocean outside the picture window.

"Remember how we used to go out every Wednesday night?"

"Yes."

"We could do that."

"Yes."

"And spend the weekends together," I said. "Like we used to?"

"That would work for me," Richie said.

"And what happens other days?" I said.

"Don't ask, don't tell."

"Think this will work?"

"We'll make it work. I can't imagine life without you either."

I rolled up onto his chest and put my lips so they brushed his.

"You're smart for a gangster," I said.

"I'm not a gangster."

"You're smart anyway," I said.

"Smarter than I was," Richie said.

Then I kissed him and closed my eyes, and the darkness was all there was.